BRIDEGROOM
ON APPROVAL

BRIDEGROOM ON APPROVAL

BY
DAY LECLAIRE

MILLS & BOON®

*First published in Great Britain 1999
Large Print edition 2000
Harlequin Mills & Boon Limited,
Eton House, 18-24 Paradise Road,
Richmond, Surrey TW9 1SR*

© Day Totton Smith 1999

ISBN 0 263 16371 7

*Set in Times Roman 16½ on 18 pt.
16-0002-49590*

*Printed and bound in Great Britain
by Antony Rowe Ltd, Chippenham, Wiltshire*

PROLOGUE

Hidden Harbor, Maryland

HANNA TYLER RESTED HER HEAD against the high-backed leather chair and closed her eyes. It had been an interminably long day and she couldn't wait for it to end. Soon, she consoled herself. Very soon. Just a few more people to see, a half dozen more papers to review and sign, five or six more family problems to settle and she'd be free to call it a day. A sense of satisfaction filled her, despite her exhaustion. It had been a good day helping the residents of Hidden Harbor, of trying, ever so slightly, to balance the scales.

A light tapping on her office door heralded the entrance of her secretary. The gruff old woman took one step inside, her stocky body blocking admittance until she'd confirmed that Hanna was receiving. ''It's Mr. DuBerry, Mrs. Tyler. Will you see him?''

''Of course, Pru. Send him in.''

5

The secretary shifted to one side, permitting a tall, handsome man entry. "Thanks, old girl," Dix said with a friendly smile.

To Hanna's amusement, her secretary's expression rearranged itself into an even more sour state, if that were possible. "You've got ten minutes and I'm timing you."

"You people and your clocks and timetables." DuBerry shook his head in bemusement. "I don't know how you do it. Or why, for that matter."

"Hello, Dix," Hanna interrupted, waving a hand to the chair in front of her. "Have a seat and tell me why you've come."

He waited until the door behind him closed before speaking. "I think you can guess," he said with a stunning smile. "Today's the day."

Without a word, she opened her desk drawer and removed a small jewelry box. Very gently, she set it in the middle of her painfully neat desk.

Dix sighed. "Ah, Hanna. I'd hoped to see that diamond on your finger. I'm disappointed in you."

She fought to maintain a composed demeanor while inside she felt like someone chiseled away at what passed for her heart. It had been going on for a long time. Tiny fractures, little breaks, a chip here and there. If something didn't change—and soon—it wouldn't be too long before she had nothing left to offer a man. Even the wrong man. "Take it," she said evenly.

Large, blond, handsome, impressive muscles rippling across his broad shoulders and he still didn't have the necessary power to touch her heart. But then... Maybe no one did, since she doubted she was capable of love. He flashed the smile that had melted many a woman—with one notable exception—and pocketed the jeweler's box. "I wish it could have been different, Hanna," he said in a woebegone voice that failed to convince her of his sincerity. Perhaps it was the choked sigh he'd incorporated into her name. Hanna with a hiccup. Just great. "I think we'd have made a fantastic pair."

"So did the last six men the boys introduced me to."

Even that didn't dent his congenial expression. "You're quite a woman. Smart, pretty... Smart."

"You mentioned that already." Perhaps she shouldn't be so rough on him. No doubt those two words encompassed the full extent of his list of adjectives.

"It could have worked."

"Because of the boys?"

"Despite them," Dix said, surprising her with his momentary acuity. "They *are* a handful, dearest. But I'd have managed."

"You do have big hands," she acknowledged.

"More than big enough to take care of you and all your problems. Come on, Hanna. Marry me. I know you don't like the fact that Jeb put me up to this. But that doesn't mean we're not right for each other."

Take care of her? Not a chance. As for Jeb... She was used to the boys interfering, since it had been going on ever since their father had died. The chair suddenly felt too soft, too accommodating. She straightened away from it, refusing to bend. "Thanks for stopping by, Dix."

"Er...Hanna?" For the first time his charming smile faltered. "I hope this won't adversely affect our other relationship."

She forced her hands to remain relaxed on the desktop. "Do I strike you as a petty person?"

He stood, his frame straining the confines of his perfectly tailored suit. "Thank you, dearest. That's most generous."

"Please don't call me that."

He must have decided he'd outstayed his welcome. Charming smile back in place, he broke for the door. It popped open just as he reached it. He stepped across the threshold, carefully avoiding Pru's scrutiny, and lumbered down the hallway with a lack of grace that had always annoyed Hanna. It was... untidy.

"Another disappointed suitor?" Pru asked, her gravelly voice filled with disgust.

"Oh, of course."

"No great loss with that one. He was all muscles and teeth without the spine to support it. He'd never have made you happy."

Still Hanna refused to relax against the back of her chair. "Why is it so difficult to find a man worth marrying? It's not like there aren't plenty to choose from. Ever since that magazine article on me broke, they're practically lined up at my door."

"You know why. It's because you can't decide whether they want you for yourself or for your ability to quadruple their bank balance."

Pru's smile took on a nasty edge. "That's what you get for being so good with money. Though I'd think those boys of yours would scare them off."

Hanna tossed aside her reading glasses, the heavy black frames clattering against the polished wood desk. "Not likely since they're the ones who keep dropping potential husbands off on my doorstep."

"That's why you should go looking someplace where they don't know you."

Go looking for a husband-to-be, when she was already knee-deep in them? No way! "What's up, Pru? I only have seven minutes until my next appointment."

Her secretary sat down, setting a padded envelope on the desk in front of Hanna. "I'm serious, my girl. If you don't open up to someone and be quick about it, soon there won't be anything of yourself left to give. You can't let fear rule you forever."

Pru's comment was so close to her own thoughts, Hanna could only stare. "You think I should open up to someone like Dix?" she finally asked, a spark of amusement easing her earlier discomfort. "You can't seriously believe he, or any of my other suitors for that matter, are here because they've fallen in love with me.''

''No, I do not. If anything that magazine article was as good as dumping a honey pot in front of a bear's den. They can't come out of hibernation fast enough to scoop you up and suck you down.'' The secretary was never one to coat her true opinion with sugar. If anything she tended to tart it up. The more bite, the more people paid attention, she liked to say. ''But that doesn't mean there isn't someone who's right for you. I even have a possible solution.''

''You're going to stop the boys from match-making?''

''No. You can do that for yourself.'' An actual smile crossed Pru's homely face. It was a rather wicked-looking baring of teeth, but still passed as a smile. ''I'm going to send you someplace where you can have your pick of husbands. Or rather, the town of Hidden Harbor is sending you. It's a place they don't know you and where you can open up without worry or suspicion.''

Hanna sat silently for a moment before shaking her head in confusion. ''The whole town is sending me?''

"Well, sort of. They don't realize where they're sending you or what you're supposed to accomplish once you're there. I used a little emotional blackmail to make everyone cough up some bucks for a birthday present. Told them you needed a break and they were going to give it to you."

"And they agreed?"

Pru's grin flashed again, even more wicked this time. "I didn't give them much choice. You forget they have to get past me to see you. And they can't make all those lovely—not to mention profitable—investments if they don't see you."

"Oh, Pru. You didn't."

"Damn right, I did. You need a companion, someone special to love and share your life with, and I aim to see you get one."

A companion, fine. But a lover? She shied from the idea. "Give me the details," Hanna said warily. "What do I have to do to find this man?"

"It's a snap. Nothing you can't handle." The secretary nodded her head toward the packet on the desk. "It's all in there."

Slowly Hanna drew the large, gold-embossed envelope closer and opened it. To her surprise, she found a white velvet pouch inside. ''More and more intriguing,'' she murmured, slipping a heavy gold wafer from the pouch. The wafer caught the sunshine streaming in the window and reflected it, throwing off shards of shimmering golden light. A card accompanied the pouch and read, *The Beaumonts wish you joy and success as you embark on your search for matrimonial happiness.*

''That gold thing's a ticket,'' Pru explained. ''See how it has 'ticket' scrawled on it in little curlicues? Makes it sort of self-explanatory. Leastwise, it would if you could read the fancy lettering.''

Hanna fought to keep a straight face. ''Sure enough.'' It truly was a beautiful piece of work for a mere ticket. She fixed her secretary with an intent look. ''Now for the million dollar question.... What's it a ticket to?''

''To a ball. If you take a peek at the other side you'll see it has 'Cinderella Ball' scribbled on it.''

Hanna frowned, flipping the gold wafer and tracing the finely etched script. ''Not quite as self-explanatory. What sort of ball is that?''

Pru hesitated, an unusual occurrence. Taking a deep breath, she confessed, "A wedding ball."

"A wedding—" Hanna broke off, shaking her head in amused disbelief. "You're kidding."

"Not even a little. It used to be hosted by an elderly couple named Montague. Now their daughter and her husband throw it. You fill in all these ridiculous forms that give detailed information about yourself and send them in."

"There's an application?"

"Probably to weed out undesirables. Once you pass the investigative process, they send you the ticket you're holding. It was even hand-delivered by a liveried messenger."

"Really?" Hanna was impressed. "That must have been expensive."

"So was the ticket."

"And this ball?" She lifted an eyebrow. "What happens there?"

"Simple. You hand over your ticket and go husband-hunting. Since it takes place in Nevada, as soon as you find the man of your dreams, you can marry. They have a county clerk there to process marriage applications and officials who tie the knot." Pru was chattering—a first since Hanna had known her. It had to mean she was nervous, uncertain of how her proposition would be received. "This year they've changed things a bit. It's a masked ball. I guess they figure it'll force people to get past the distraction of physical appearance and focus on personality. Asinine proposition, in my opinion, but what the hell." She paused for a breath. "So? What do you think?"

"I think it sounds totally insane."

"Oh." Pru looked crushed. "You hate it, don't you?"

"Actually, I'm intrigued." Hanna hesitated, analyzing the possibilities. "No one would know me there. Right?"

"Not a chance, especially with your mask on. You could relax and see what happens. Let nature take its course. And if you don't meet someone? Hell, you'd be no worse off than you are now."

A fierce longing seized hold, the need to be loved for herself so strong it became a physical ache. *Don't be ridiculous,* she ordered herself sternly. She didn't want love. She wanted a man who'd be the perfect companion, someone she could trust, who would offer stability and intellectual stimulus. She didn't need emotion. It didn't last, nor was it safe. "What if I find someone?"

"You bring home a husband. Or you can hook up with some willing soul and bring him home to try out for a time. If nothing else, having a man in tow would stymie the boys." Pru leaned across the desk. "But you make sure he's a strong one, Hanna girl. Not another of those useless charmers the boys keep parading under your nose. Charm ain't worth squat when your back's up against the wall."

"Someone who can love me for me and who's strong instead of charming." Hanna shook her head. "That's a tall order."

"I have a feeling about this. And my feelings are always right on the money. He'll be there. All you have to do is keep looking until you find him."

San Francisco, California

Marc Salvatore waited until his eldest brother, Luc, ran out of arguments. Then he offered a charming smile, along with a distinctly Latin shrug—a graceful movement of his shoulders that warned his five brothers that he wouldn't be swayed no matter how hard they might try.

"For the last time, I'm telling you the ticket to the Cinderella Ball is a joke. Rafe and I have a meeting scheduled this week which happens to coincide with this party he and his wife are throwing. The Beaumonts are aware I'm single. You know Rafe's sense of humor. Take it from there."

"No," his twin, Stefano, cut in. "We don't know Beaumont's sense of humor. He's *your* business contact. All we know about him is that he grows excellent coffee beans which make even more excellent coffee."

"Well… And he has a wife who's clearly insane," Luc added in a dry tone.

"Ella isn't crazy," Marc objected mildly, continuing with his packing. "She's just a dedicated matchmaker."

"And throws these marriage balls to prove it?"

Marc shrugged again. "A family tradition. You should understand that, considering our Salvatore heritage."

"Are you attending the ball? Is that why you're calling on Beaumont this particular

weekend?'' Stef demanded. ''Are you planning to find yourself a wife?''

Marc zipped his suitcase closed and turned
to confront his brothers. He folded his arms
across his chest and struggled to suppress the
quixotic sense of humor that so often caused
him trouble with his brothers. ''I have about
as much chance of getting married Saturday
night as Luc had of becoming engaged to a
beautiful preacher's daughter disguised as a
dowdy secretary in order to protect his infant
niece from the clutches of the child welfare
people.''

Stef grinned, his sense of humor as skewed
as his brother's. ''Now what are the odds of
that happening?''

''Too damned good!'' Luc practically
roared. ''Since that's how Grace and I became
engaged.''

Marc snapped his fingers, his eyes widening
in mock horror. ''That's right. And if memory
serves, you were all set to marry her, too. For
the sake of the baby.''

A dangerous light flickered in Luc's eyes.
''I loved Grace or I'd never have married
her.''

Marc's grin lit up his face. "Exactly, big brother. And why? I'll tell you. Because marriage is a serious business. Too serious to be decided in a single night. Have you forgotten? Salvatores marry once. And it's always for love. One of these days I'll meet the woman I'm meant to share the rest of my life with. When that happens, I'll get my ring on her finger as fast as she'll allow and make her the happiest woman in the world."

"I'm relieved to hear you say that," Luc muttered, apparently mollified. "The trouble is you're always thinking with your heart. It's going to get you into trouble one of these days. Especially where women are concerned."

Marc lowered his gaze. "Yes, it's a serious failing," he confessed morosely. "But cheer up. What are the odds that I'll meet the one woman I can't live without at this Cinderella Ball?" He didn't give them time to respond. Picking up his suitcase, he walked out the door.

"What are the odds? Damn, but I wish he'd stop asking that," Stef muttered. "He's got to be tempting the fates. If they have as perverse a sense of humor as Marco, we may have a new sister by next week.''

Luc released a heavy sigh. ''I'd say we can count on it.''

CHAPTER ONE

The Beaumonts' Cinderella Ball—Forever, Nevada

TAKE A BREATH! Hanna silently ordered herself, struggling to hang on to her self-control. It was difficult. She'd never felt so out of her element in all of her twenty-six years. Not that she'd ever betray that fact. Not a chance. She'd spent a lifetime tackling events and situations that weren't of her own making. And she'd handled each of them with every scrap of skill she could muster.

She could handle a simple marriage ball, as well. No problem.

Glancing at her watch, she nodded in satisfaction. Eight o'clock on the dot, just as the invitation had stated. Perfect. Paying off the cab driver, she stepped from the back of the taxi with all the grace of a woman wearing a ball gown and tiara instead of dressed in a costume resembling a plucked chicken. Perhaps attending the masked ball as a swan princess

21

hadn't been the best choice, after all. The feathers tickled and the gold net she'd employed to restrain her hair had clearly failed in its duty. Auburn ringlets were already escaping, trembling at her temples and at the nape of her neck. She almost turned and fled to the relative safety of the cab. But at the last instant, she did the same as always when faced with an obstacle that caused uncertainty and fear.

She forced her posture into painful stiffness and confronted it dead-on, jaw set, gaze unflinching, and fears buried so deep they'd never be unearthed.

A group of party-goers passed by, no doubt anxious to get to the business of finding a mate. Immediately she felt better. A plump Juliet, an aging Cinderella, a painfully nervous Sleeping Beauty and a woman who had the audacity to attend as Lady Godiva joined the stream of visitors heading for the Beaumont mansion. One silk-and-feathered swan no longer seemed the least outrageous.

Checking to be certain her mask covered her face—offering a protection she secretly appreciated—she walked toward the double doors leading into the mansion. Once inside, she looked around in amazement. It was quite a place. The marble entrance hall seemed to stretch into infinity, the huge support pillars decorated with lush pine garland, twinkling fairy lights and white satin bows. A massive chandelier, glittering with thousands of tiny prisms, caught the setting sun and scattered a dancing circle of rainbows in what some might consider a promise of irresistible hope.

She tried to skirt the rainbows, but if she didn't know better, she'd swear they sought her out, dancing across her white silk-and-lace costume and catching in her eyes. She hastened deeper into the hall where twin staircases curved upward to the second-floor ballroom, joining to form a perfect heart. It drew her forward, sparking an excitement that overrode her nervousness.

A reception line formed at the top of the steps, hosted by a tall, striking man and a gorgeous, dark-haired woman. They had to be the Beaumonts and, without question, they were the most simply garbed of all. He'd dressed in a black tux, while his wife wore a floor-length gold sheath. At their feet romped a three-year-old boy, his miniature tux rumpled and his flaming red bow tie askew. He grinned at her from beneath a mop of dark curls, his amber-tinted eyes glittering with unmistakable mischief.

She grinned back, relaxing for the first time in days. Since the line had ground to a halt, she stooped to talk to him, shoving her feathered mask on top of her head. "Hey, there, buster."

"My name isn't Buster," he informed her with a trace of scorn. "That's my friend's name. Buster and Chick. They're my bestest buddies. I'm Donato. I got named after my grandpa."

"It's a lovely name," Hanna assured gravely.

He reached out with a cautious hand and touched one of her feathers. "You look pretty. Whatcha being?"

It took an instant to understand his question. "Oh! I guess I'm a swan princess."

"I seen that story. You have to be a swan until the prince says he loves you. Right?"

"I'm not sure," she confessed. "I just liked the costume."

Interesting she'd made this particular character choice when she'd learned long ago not to indulge in the fantasy that went along with it. She'd been trained from childhood to take care of herself and she'd been putting that training into practice for years now. No doubt, she'd continue to do so until the end of her days. Besides, she didn't *really* need love. She was a strong, capable woman who didn't require a man to make her life complete.

So what was she doing here? a cynical inner voice demanded. The question had been flirting in the far recesses of her mind and her mouth curved into a self-mocking smile as she acknowledged its validity. She knew what she'd been telling herself.... She was searching for companionship. Nothing more. Someone to talk to, to share her day and hold her close during the endless nights. Someone she could lo— Her hands closed into fists. Someone she could relate to on an intellectual level.

She caught a sudden movement out of the corner of her eyes. Glancing up she noticed a man standing in the shadows beyond the reception line. He was even more attractive than her host. Perhaps not quite as tall, but he had a lean, athletic build that appealed. The muscular strength evident beneath his black shirt wasn't the same as the excessive weight-lifting that had sculpted Dix DuBerry's body. Instead it spoke of swift action and whipcord strength. A smile touched her mouth.

This man wouldn't lumber gracelessly down a hallway.

He responded to her appraisal with a nod and, realizing she'd been staring, she looked swiftly away. What in the world had gotten into her? Okay, so his shoulders were deliciously broad, his eyes as appealing as a forbidden dollop of hot fudge and his smile as enticing as any she'd ever seen. He obviously wasn't here to find a wife or he'd be wearing a costume. That meant he was off-limits. Unable to resist, she glanced at him again. If she'd been a different type of woman, she'd have shielded the look with her lashes. But she'd always confronted the various aspects of her life head-on and she wasn't about to change because of this man.

He was still staring, his scrutiny so unmistakable, her earlier nervousness returned in a rush. Did he recognize her? Had he read the article about her business acumen? Slipping her mask back in place, she returned her attention to the little boy. ''It's been nice talking to you,'' Hanna said.

''Did you come here to get married?''

"Maybe. I'd need to meet someone very special first." Someone as special as the man standing behind the young boy.

"You gotta give your ticket to my Aunt Shayne." He pointed to an attractive blonde at the end of the line. "They won't let you in if you don't give her a ticket."

"Thank you. I'll do that."

He stuck out his hand. "Wanna shake? I got taught how."

"I sure do." She took his hand in hers, impressed by his firm shake. "Nice meeting you, Donato."

The line had moved forward and Hanna straightened, turning to greet her hostess. "Hello." She offered her hand for a second time. "Hanna Tyler."

"Welcome. I'm Ella Beaumont." She glanced at the little boy crouched at her feet and smiled. "I see you've met my son."

"He's adorable."

"Thank you." Eyes identical to Donato's reflected wry amusement. "We think so, but we're a bit prejudiced."

"Understandable."

Ella touched her husband's arm, drawing his attention. "Rafe, this is Hanna Tyler."

"It's a pleasure to meet you." He inclined his head in a courtly manner and took her hand in his. "Good luck this evening. I hope you find someone very special."

"Thank you. I'll do my best."

He indicated a slender blond woman at his side. "If you'll give your ticket to my sister, Shayne, she'll explain how the ball works."

Hanna gave a final nod and turned toward Shayne. Huge, dark eyes regarded her with a friendly expression. "Welcome to the Cinderella Ball," she said.

"Thank you. It's a beautiful place."

"Isn't it? Perfect for such a romantic purpose." She took Hanna's ticket and dropped it into the velvet-lined basket she held. "The ground and ballroom levels are available to visitors. So feel free to explore anywhere on those two floors. The rest, I'm afraid, is off-limits. You'll find a banquet available downstairs and the gardens are particularly pleasant this evening. They can be reached through the dining area."

"And once I find someone..." Hanna hesitated, unable to assume finding a partner was inevitable, despite the purpose of the evening. "*If* I find someone? What then?"

''The marriage ceremonies are conducted in the salons off the main ballroom. We offer a variety of services, and if you've any questions or problems during your stay, footmen are stationed in all the rooms. They're wearing gold-and-white uniforms, so you can't miss them.'' Shayne's smile came with a natural generosity Hanna found irresistible. ''Now be sure to have a wonderful evening. And good luck finding the perfect partner.''

Perfect? Hanna suppressed a sigh. Not likely. She'd be happy if she could find someone who found her interesting for herself, instead of who she was and what she could do for him. ''Thank you, Shayne. I'll try.''

Unable to help herself, Hanna glanced once more in the direction of her mystery man. To her disappointment, he'd gone. The pang his disappearance stirred caught her by surprise. It also worried her. Emotions had no part in what would transpire this evening. That would be a mistake. Better this particular man take his irresistible smile elsewhere. The partner she chose would attract her intellectually, not sexually. His emotions and thoughts would be as precise and controlled as possible.

She glanced at her watch and frowned. It was eight-thirty already. She'd wasted a lot of time mooning over a man totally wrong for her purposes. If she didn't get a move on the best choices would be snatched up. And she needed every minute of the next few hours to make sure the man she selected met her list of requirements.

But perhaps it wouldn't prove as difficult as she'd anticipated. After all, he'd be a companion, not a lover, a man of academic rather than emotional inclination. That was what she wanted, right? By utilizing a bit of logic and a standard process of elimination, it would be a snap.

She gave an emphatic nod that loosened a few more disobedient curls. One intellectual, heavy on brainpower and light on love, coming up.

Marc Salvatore stood on a balcony high above the ballroom, his shoulder propped against a snow-white pillar. He felt as though he hung above a fairyland, white twinkling lights and greenery adding to the otherworldly impression. For a while the swirl of color and movement dazzled the eye. But after a time, he found his gaze returning again and again to a petite redhead dressed in ivory—the woman who'd caught his eye in the reception line.

Her hair was a deep auburn, the rich strands several shades paler around her face, like a perfect sunset reflecting on a pure sea of snow. She'd confined the heavy curls in some sort of golden net, as though in an attempt to tame their exuberance. But little ringlets escaped her mastery and danced around her huge feathered mask. More feathers decorated her costume, accenting an enchanting confection of lace and silk that made him think she'd come as a swan princess. Except for the minuscule straps that held her dress together, her shoulders were bare and seemed to glitter with gold dust. Her dress caught the light, as well, sequins or tiny glass diamonds splintering into rainbows with her every movement. Not that she moved often. No doubt that had been part of what attracted his attention, her stillness in the center of a storm of activity. And yet, the few times her body escaped the tight control she exerted, she became a miniature whirlwind of physical expression.

She had an elegance that appealed, her body slender yet shapely with legs that were absolutely breathtaking. If circumstances had been different, he'd have swept down, removed her from her circle of admirers and taken her off somewhere private in order to follow up on those glances they'd exchanged in the reception line. *If* circumstances had been different.

A soft rustle of skirts sounded behind him and he caught a distinctive whiff of perfume. "Hello, Shayne," he said without turning around.

"Clever man," she teased. "Or is it that you can sense any time a woman's around?"

He reluctantly switched his attention from the redhead. "What can I say?" he confessed with a shrug. "It's a Salvatore trait."

"And we poor women don't stand a chance?"

He fought to suppress a grin. "Consider yourself warned."

"Why aren't you downstairs enjoying the festivities?" she asked.

"I'm content to watch from here. Besides, I'm not looking for a wife." He gave Rafe's sister his full regard, as captivated by her beauty tonight as he'd been at their first meeting. She wore her honey-blond hair in a formal twist at the nape of her neck, a constrained style that belied the passion inherent in her vivid dark eyes. "Nor am I dressed appropriately."

"That's not a problem. I have something you can use." She pulled her hands from behind her back, dangling a sheathed sword and belt in front of him. "I brought this for you in case you wanted to play."

He tilted his head to one side and regarded her with amused suspicion. "Were you the one who sent the ticket?"

Her eyes sparkled with mischief. "And if I was?"

"Are you trying to tempt me?"

"Yes." She smiled, enhancing her natural allure. Not that she was aware of it.

Shayne seemed uniquely oblivious to her own attraction. He'd have done something to change that except he wasn't in the market for either a lover or a bride, despite how he'd teased his brothers. With Shayne, he didn't doubt, it would have to be the latter. She struck him as an all-or-nothing type of woman. Added to that minor inconvenience, Rafe had put out clear signals. His little sister was off-limits. And Marc had too much respect for Rafe to take advantage of his hospitality.

"I appreciate the thought." Marc gestured toward the sword. "But it wouldn't be fair to play since I have no intention of paying the ultimate price. The women attending the Cinderella Ball want marriage."

"True." She regarded him curiously. "Are you sure you wouldn't want it, too, if you found the right woman downstairs?"

The right woman... For some reason his thoughts turned to the redhead and he sighed in regret. "Tempting. But, no."

"Are you certain?" Shayne set the sword against the pillar next to him. "You wouldn't like to go downstairs for a little while and see if Cupid strikes?"

"Quite certain, thank you." He caught her chin in the crook of his index finger and lifted her face to his. "What about you? You've gone out of your way to find me a bride.... Are you interested in finding a husband?"

For a brief instant her lips trembled before firming. "I did that once," she confessed in a low voice. "There won't be a second time."

Regret filled him. "My apologies," he said, releasing her. He wasn't often so clumsy with women. Nor would he deliberately cause such distress. "That was careless of me."

She shrugged, turning to stare out at the dancers twirling across the floor where the costumes created a kaleidoscope of vibrant color. "You weren't to know."

"If it makes you feel any better, he was a fool to lose a woman like you," Marc offered gently.

"He didn't lose me." The yearning in her voice was painful to hear. If he didn't sense it would be a mistake, he'd take her in his arms and offer the only comfort he could in a situation such as this. "I was young and foolish. We never had a chance to discover whether or not it would have worked."

"Perhaps sometime in the future you'll have another chance with him?"

"It's unlikely." She bowed her head. "A few years ago, perhaps. But not any longer. I'm not the woman I was."

"There's not a man on this planet who wouldn't want the woman you've become. Shayne…" He waited until she glanced over her shoulder at him. Waited until she'd accepted the sincerity in his eyes. "What you need to decide is whether or not he's worth having in your life again."

"And if he is?"

"Follow him to the ends of the earth," Marc advised. "Show him what he lost when your relationship ended. Make him fight to take you back."

"Is that what you'd do?"

It didn't require any thought. "If I found that sort of love, I'd never allow anyone or anything to get in my way. I'd fight for her, protect and cherish her. And I'd love her every day I drew breath. She'd never know a moment's doubt about how I felt." He smiled to lighten the mood. "What can I say? It's how I was raised."

"May I tell you something, Mr. Salvatore?" She linked arms with him, her smile restored. "The woman you marry will be very lucky."

He returned his attention to the festivities far below…and to a certain striking redhead surrounded by a group of eager admirers. "No, my sweet. Finding such a love would make me a very lucky man."

Hanna smiled into yet another friendly face, but her enthusiasm had started to flag. She'd met so many men and had enjoyed talking to each and every one of them. She'd determinedly been herself since it seemed only fair—slipping cautiously from beneath the tight yoke of control that so often governed her actions and allowing a more natural vivaciousness to take hold. It had worked too well. She'd had her pick of men—young, old, smart, less-than-brilliant. She only had to select one that met her lengthy list of criteria and she'd have what she'd always wanted. A husband to come home to when the days were long and the nights unbearably lonely.

Only one thing stopped her.

The process seemed so cold. Despite telling herself she didn't want emotion intruding on a companionable relationship, she also couldn't see any of the men she'd met so far sitting in her living room, let alone tucked up in her bed. In fact, the idea of any of them touching her in an intimate manner filled her with such nervous dread, it was a wonder she could string two coherent words together.

All around her the party glittered, the laughter bright and merry. But behind her mask, an inescapable pain and longing took hold. Pru had meant well. But clearly, it wasn't meant to be. Hanna wasn't Cinderella destined to find her prince. At least, not this night.

"Excuse me," she finally murmured to the men surrounding her. "I'll return in a few minutes." Before anyone could stop her, she darted through a narrow opening in her circle of admirers and escaped into the crowd.

Somewhere nearby the clock struck midnight and Hanna couldn't suppress a smile at the irony. She felt like Cinderella fleeing the ball, turning from a beautiful princess back into a common cinder girl. Or in her case, from a mysterious swan princess into a simple duckling.

She left the ballroom and headed downstairs. One of the rooms offered a huge banquet with every conceivable delicacy available, but she wasn't in the least hungry. Beyond a set of French doors the gardens beckoned, offering peace and quiet and a welcoming solitude. She followed the pathways until she found a bench beneath a large tree, one mercifully absent of fairy lights. Taking a seat, she tucked her knees close against her chest and wrapped her arms around her legs.

"This was a big mistake," she announced to the world at large. Then to her horror, she did something she couldn't remember ever doing before.

She burst into tears.

Marc watched his pretty redhead flee her circle of admirers. They might not realize she was running away, but he knew it with a bone-deep certainty. He didn't hesitate. Snatching up the belt and sword Shayne had provided, he secured it to his waist. He took the stairs leading from the balcony to the ballroom floor, arriving in time to see his swan princess dart down the next flight of stairs leading toward the dining area. A woman dressed in a stunning black gown blocked his path. He couldn't quite place which romantic figure she represented, but it didn't matter. She had something he needed.

For the first time, he blessed his father for the Italian lessons Dom had insisted were a vital part of his sons' education. *"Signorina,"* he said, executing a graceful bow. "I believe your costume is the most beautiful I've seen so far tonight."

The accent worked like a charm. She blushed, deep dimples flickering to life in her cheeks. "If I hadn't already found the perfect man, I'd ask you to dance."

"A shame. For if I had not found the perfect woman, I'd have happily accepted." He hesitated. "May I make one small suggestion in regard to your dress?"

A tiny frown puckered her brow. "Well... sure."

He caught the end of the black scarf encircling her neck and gently pulled the strip of silk. It slipped along her throat like a lover's caress. "This is an unnecessary distraction. You should not hide such a neck and shoulders."

She swallowed. "Do you really think so?"

"*Senza dubbio.* Without doubt." Actually, it was the absolute truth, or he'd never have said such a thing. "Would you mind if I kept your scarf?" He shrugged. "I'd claim I wanted it for a memento, but the truth is, I wish to use it as a mask for the ball."

She offered him a sympathetic smile. "Did you forget yours?"

"I'm afraid so."

"Take it. I'm happy to help." She turned to go, then hesitated. "Oh! And good luck with your lady."

Marc smiled. "And you with your man."

He didn't waste any more time, but darted down the steps to the banquet room. A quick scan of the crowd confirmed that his little redhead wasn't among the diners. Selecting a steak knife from one of the tables, he swiftly slit holes in the scarf and tied it around his head. Simple, but effective, he decided. Between the mask and the sword Shayne had provided, he could pass as Zorro or some similar type romantic swashbuckler.

Now to find his swan princess.

It had gotten late enough that the gardens were fairly deserted. He roamed the paths with swift efficiency, finally slipping up on a splash of white silk and feathers on a bench tucked well beneath a large sycamore tree. She was crying, he realized in alarm. Nothing bothered him quite as much as a woman in distress and for some odd reason this woman's distress disturbed him more than was normal. No doubt it had something to do with his attraction for her. But he also sensed this wasn't a woman easily reduced to tears. Not giving himself time to think, he slipped to the far side of the tree, grasped the lowest branch and swung himself upward.

Easing the sword from its scabbard, he grasped one of the trailing ends of his black scarf and sliced off a square. To his amusement, he noticed that a bit of dainty lace dec-

orated the end. Perfect. Skewering the improvised handkerchief on the tip of the sword, he
slowly lowered it toward his weeping princess.

''For you, *Signorina*,'' he said quietly, hoping he wouldn't startle her too badly.

Her head jerked up and her breath hitched
in surprise. ''Who's there?'' she demanded.

''No one of importance,'' he said with a
shrug, flavoring his words with the gentlest of
Italian accents. ''Just a man sitting in a tree
watching a beautiful swan leak tears all over
her feathers.''

A smile trembled on her lips and she
reached for the scrap of silk and lace. ''Thank
you, but I'm not crying,'' she lied with a bla-
tancy that defied argument. ''I never cry.''

She fell silent for a minute, no doubt struggling to regain her composure and control her
nonexistent tears. He didn't mind. He was a
patient man, one of the few Salvatores who
could claim such a virtue. A good thing. He
sensed he'd stumbled across a woman who
found control a vital component when con-
fronting those entering her world.

''Why are you sitting in that tree?'' she finally asked.

He'd been right. Gone was the vulnerable woman of moments before and in her place was a woman of strength and determination. It made for an interesting contrast. ''I quite like trees,'' he said after a moment's contemplation. ''I always have. They make excellent places from which to swoop.''

A smile flirted with her mouth again. ''Swoop?''

''Yes, swoop. Shall I demonstrate?''

Securing his sword, he grasped one of the larger branches and swung high over her bench. At the last instant, he released his grasp and executed a quick midair somersault, dropping lightly in a crouch beside her. It was a maneuver that would have done Errol Flynn proud. It was also a maneuver that had broken his arm when he'd worked on perfecting it at the great age of ten.

She looked appropriately impressed. ''You like how I swoop?'' he asked, keeping his Italian accent intact.

''Very impressive.''

He continued to crouch beside her, balancing easily on the balls of his feet. ''So tell me what has made you cry, *Signorina.* Perhaps I can help.''

She shook her head. "Thank you, but I don't think there's anything anyone can do for me."

"You must have thought a husband and marriage would help or you wouldn't be here," he argued logically. "Now, why would someone as beautiful as you need to come to a Cinderella Ball to find a husband? I would think you'd have men lined up at your door."

Apparently, he'd said the wrong thing. She withdrew into herself, her back stiff, her chin elevated, her eyes behind the feathered mask flashing a warning even the darkness couldn't conceal. "What makes you think I'm beautiful?"

"You may wish you were not, *carissima,* but you can't hide it." Ever so gently he reached out and plucked the flamboyant mask from her face. "Not even with this."

She was as lovely as he remembered. It was almost too dark now to see the exact shade of her eyes, but he recalled they were an intriguing combination of green and gold and glittered with intelligence and character. Her character was also expressed in the clean, strong lines of her face. Her nose was straight, her jaw firm, her cheekbones high and broad. In the absence of light, her ivory dress and pale skin had a translucent glow, like the rich texture of a black-and-white movie, her hair and lips glimmering with the only hint of color, a vibrant red that even the darkness couldn't subdue.

"You shouldn't have done that," she informed him in a steely voice.

Did she think he'd find her tone intimidating? She had a lot to learn. But she would...he'd see to it. Personally. "Why not? It's after midnight." He fixed her with a steady regard. "I suspect the time for fun and games is past. Don't you?"

"I was never very good at games." She shrugged. "At least, not the kind men and women play."

"Why don't we dispense with the games?" He dropped his accent, a fact she acknowledged with an uplifted eyebrow. Straddling the bench, he asked, "Why are you here?"

"To find a husband."

"I assumed as much." He put a hint of steel in his own voice. "You're evading the question, though. Why did you come here to do your husband-hunting?"

"The usual reasons, I guess."

"Ah, *cara,*" he murmured. "If you play games, so shall I."

She held up her hands. "Okay, okay. You can drop the phony accent."

"It's not so phony. I'm first generation American, raised to take pride in my Italian heritage." Unable to resist touching her, he hooked her chin and tipped her face up to his. "You strike me as a direct sort of woman. Tell me why you're really here."

"To find a husband…"

"And?"

"Look… Maybe this would be easier if we knew each other's names." She offered her hand, forcing him to release her chin. "I'm Hanna Tyler."

He took her hand in his, not in the least surprised by the firmness of her grip. "Marc Salvatore."

"Learning your name was supposed to make me feel more comfortable." Her mouth tilted to one side. "For some reason it doesn't."

"It's the forced intimacy of the situation. You have one night to find a partner. You arrived masked so the participants aren't distracted by appearance and can find personalities that mesh, rather than relying on physical appeal alone. On top of that you're expected to expose your most secret longings to complete strangers. Somehow I suspect you're not comfortable with that.''

''Is it that obvious?''

''It is to me.'' He frowned in thought. ''I'll tell you what... I'll leave my mask on for now and you tell me why you've come and the sort of man you hoped to find.''

''That hardly seems fair,'' she commented drily. ''You know what I look like, but I'm left in the dark.''

He smiled at her inadvertent pun. ''If we're able to reach an understanding, I'll take it off and we'll go from there. But if at any point you want to end the conversation, say the word and I'll walk away. You've opened up to a stranger, someone you'll never see again and who will never reveal a word of what you've said. You can't even be embarrassed if our paths should cross, since you won't know it's me. Perhaps it'll be easier that way.''

She gave his suggestion careful consideration. ''So I'm supposed to tell you my life story?''

''No strings attached. No judgements. No expectations. You're in complete control.''

She looked directly at him and in that moment Marc knew that he'd lied to his brothers. He had found love. He'd found it where he'd least expected and least wanted to find it. But he was a Salvatore, destined to love only one woman for the duration of his life. And because of that, he'd do something he'd never thought a sane man would do.

He'd meet and marry a woman all in one night.

CHAPTER TWO

"I'M IN COMPLETE CONTROL?" Hanna asked, her wariness clear.

"Absolutely," Marc assured. "I'm not here to give you a hard time. I'm here to help."

"Help?" A tiny frown formed between her brows. "Why? What's in it for you?"

It was a telling question and one that saddened him. Did most people she dealt with have an ulterior motive? She obviously didn't have the love and support of a family like the Salvatores or she wouldn't ask such a question. "That's up to you. For now I plan to enjoy a pleasant hour talking to you. Just easy, casual conversation."

She sighed. "Not so casual if I dump my life story on you."

"Then it won't be casual," he said with a shrug. "My shoulders can carry quite a load. Feel free to dump away." That won a smile. "So you're here to find a husband. Mind if I ask why?"

49

"The usual reasons."

Did she realize how evasive she sounded? "What are the usual reasons?" he prompted.

Her control slipped and she spun from her seat in a swirl of feathers. "I'm tired of being alone. I'd like companionship, someone who has the same interests." She glanced over her shoulder at him. "Is that too much to ask?"

Too much? "If anything, it's too little," he replied. "Do you *just* want a husband with the same interests?" He followed her into the darkness, aware that the night bound them together, cloaking them from the rest of the world and intensifying their reaction to one another. "Sounds boring. Don't you also want someone who shares your most private thoughts? Someone with whom you can express your hopes and fears, knowing that person will be there for you?"

She paused, slowly turning to face him. Her gaze reflected a deep yearning, a longing he doubted she even realized she felt. "Possibly," she admitted. "In time. If our relationship is successful."

He'd never met a woman so tightly furled, so afraid to reach out to a fellow human being.

No doubt she'd been badly burned in the past, like Shayne. And while he hadn't been able to help Rafe's sister or offer the comfort she so badly needed, he sure as hell could help Hanna. In fact, he'd be only too happy to make it his life's work. "If you married, your husband would expect a certain level of intimacy. And I don't just mean in your bed. I mean in your life."

Her feathers exploded into motion as she resumed her pacing. "Yes, I know."

"Do you?" He suspected she wasn't being honest with him. Hell, he doubted she was being honest with herself. He caught her arm, forcing her to face him again while at the same time forcing her to face his questions. "Are you willing to offer that?"

"If I trusted him."

Another telling remark. "So you came here hoping to find a man who could provide this companionship?"

"Yes."

"Why didn't you find anyone capable of that?" he questioned gently. "There are plenty of men to choose from."

"None were right."

"And what would make them right for you?"

She moistened her lips, a movement he found so erotic, it took every ounce of self-control to refrain from kissing her. She must have realized how much she'd given away with her nervous pacing, for she resumed her seat on the bench, perching on the edge as though prepared to take flight at the first hint of danger. "He'd need to be intelligent."

"A man who could conduct a rational conversation. Makes sense to me." The ringlets surrounding her face beckoned. Considering he was a mere man, how could he resist? He sat next to her, snaring the teasing curls with a finger, smiling when they coiled tightly around him. The entrapper became the entrapped. "What more would you want in a man, swan princess?"

Her hazel eyes were so pale and clear they reflected every thought and emotion for the world to see. It was a contradiction that appealed, her extreme caution at odds with what he hoped was a more natural candor. No doubt if she were aware of the transparency of her gaze, she'd find a way to shield it. For what those lovely eyes betrayed was the unmistakable flicker of desire. It provided an irresistible allure. Marc leaned forward and captured her mouth in a fleeting kiss. Her gasp of protest rippled through him before dying a welcome death. Then her lips softened and parted, offering a brief taste of unbearable sweetness.

Far, far too brief a taste.

Hanna's breath caught and she attempted to pull back. Not that she retreated far. He still held her secure in his hands, her curls resisting her efforts to free herself. "Please, let go," she whispered.

He carefully slipped his fingers from their silken snares. "Is physical attraction on your list?" he asked. "Because I'd say we had that base covered, as well."

She didn't bother with false denials, he gave her credit for that. But her mouth firmed and she gathered her impressive control around her with such swift ease, he knew it had to be a natural defense mechanism. His princess hid within a heavily guarded fortress, one that would take all his skill and determination to breach. "That still leaves one more element," she stated.

"The heart," he said in complete understanding. "You want a man who touches your
heart and soul, who you'd want today and tomorrow and next week and next year. I know
the feeling."

Her curiosity must have gotten the better of
her. "You've loved like that?" she asked.

"Not me, unfortunately. But my parents did.
And my two brothers and their wives share an
enduring love."

"Lucky them."

He smiled at her undisguised envy. "Did
you really expect to find that here in just one
night?"

"I didn't expect to find it at all," she
claimed coolly.

A dry breeze from off the desert washed
over her and, finding her the proverbial im-
movable object, it settled for creating havoc
where it could—tumbling curls and fluttering
feathers and tossing her silk dress about her
thighs. Marc shifted to provide a wind block,
though if he were honest he'd admit he liked
her on the rumpled side. It helped ease her
untouchable demeanor.

"What else could you want, if not love?" he asked.

She slanted him a swift look, one that warned that he wouldn't like her response. "You assumed that was the last item on my list, but it isn't. I'm not even sure love really exists. If it did—" She broke off with a shrug.

"You'd have found it before tonight?"

She bowed her head, her vulnerability painful to behold. She reminded him of a vibrant red rose bent beneath a force too powerful to repel. "Yes."

"Tell me the last item you're looking for."

"Honesty." Her gaze swept upward, fastening on him with fierce intensity. "I want a man who won't lie to me, who'll keep his word no matter what."

"And you've never found a man with all those characteristics, a man you could also love? I'm almost afraid to ask what you've found instead."

"I don't mind telling you. I've found affection, comradery, appreciation. And with one man I experienced respect and kindness."

"Dim reflections of the real thing."

She grew still, centered once again while an emotional storm raged around her, never quite touching her, but a threat to her stability, nonetheless. ''I'll take your word for it.''

''Is that why you came here?'' Marc demanded. ''To see if you could discover more than reflections?''

''You ask a lot of questions, considering I'm the one supposedly in control.''

''You're in control. You can answer or not, your choice.'' He didn't give her time to think that over and come to any unfortunate decisions. Instead, he hit her with another question. ''Why haven't you found love back home?''

She hesitated and he suspected she was mulling over how to phrase her response. It would seem he'd fallen for a cautious woman—one with secrets she wasn't prepared to fully reveal. Understandable. He had a secret or two of his own.

''There've been men interested in marrying me.''

''And why didn't it work?''

''I wasn't interested in marrying them. I think they appealed to my family more than to me.''

"What about the ones that did appeal to you?"

"My family discouraged them." Her jaw set. "With justification, I later learned."

"If they were so easily intimidated by your family, they couldn't have loved you."

"I told you. Love didn't come into it."

Why the hell not? he wanted to ask. Figuring discretion would be the wisest course on this particular topic, he let it go. For now. "And so you decided to attend the Beaumonts' ball and see if you couldn't find a man who would marry you without your family's interference. Is that it?"

"Yes."

It was such a simple response, but he suspected it hid a very complex set of problems. "Why would your family interfere?"

She hesitated and again he was struck with the certainty that she walked a fine line between discretion and frankness. "They think they know what's best for me. The also like how our life currently works. They don't want it to change."

"And if you marry, they're afraid it will?"

"Depending on the man...yes."

Tough. Hanna needed a change. Badly. And if that caused problems with her family, he'd deal with them. Personally. "It sounds like the man you choose for a husband would have to be strong."

"Very strong."

"And he'd have to be a man capable of commitment in the face of adversity."

"Tough, yet devoted," she agreed.

"Most of all, he'd have to be a man able to love you despite the problems he'll confront."

Her laugh held a trace of sorrow. "I already told you. Love's not on my list. Besides, it would take a miracle to find a man capable of all that. And I know better than to ask for so much."

"Perhaps this is the season for miracles."

"What are you saying?"

His sense of humor got the better of him and he laughed. "I do believe I'm offering to marry you. To fight your family for you, to offer my strength and my devotion."

"And love?"

He hesitated. "Sorry. I'm not offering that, just yet."

"Why?"

"Because you're not ready to accept it. Not after such a short acquaintance."

"You're right. If you said you loved me, I wouldn't believe you."

A shame. But if she accepted his proposal, there'd be plenty of time to convince her otherwise. "Do you accept, swan princess?"

"Take off your mask, first."

Without a word, he untied the scarf and allowed it to fall to the bench between them. Her swift inhalation told him he appealed. With luck, he more than appealed. "Well?"

She looked away, staring out into the night. "You'll do. But then, I suspect you already knew that."

"I'm not a vain man."

"You're the one in the reception line, aren't you?"

"Yes."

"I...I noticed you."

It was the second time she'd revealed her vulnerability that evening. First her tears and now her hesitant admission. He suspected most people didn't see her lower her guard once, let alone twice. "I noticed you, too."

"This could be a terrible mistake."

"If it is, we'll correct it." He leaned forward and caught her hand in his. "But what if it isn't? What if fate or destiny intended us to meet?"

Her mouth twisted. "Or what if we're a pair of fools caught up in the romance of the night?"

He suppressed a sigh, regretting that someone so young and lovely should be so cynical. "Then we'll be foolish together."

"And pay the consequences tomorrow?"

His sense of humor returned and he grinned, encouraging her to join in the sheer absurdity of their situation. "I can't help but think they'll be sweet consequences."

"Would you... Would you kiss me again?"

"My pleasure."

Ever so gently he pulled her into his arms. She fit beautifully, as though she'd been made as a perfect counter for him. Her arms slipped around his neck, clinging. For a long moment she stared into his eyes, searching for something he doubted she could name. He sat quietly beneath her scrutiny, allowing her to look her fill. After all, he had nothing to hide.

Satisfied, she lifted her mouth to his. Determined to be the perfect gentleman, he kissed her. He'd meant for it to be a light, tender caress. It was a foolish hope. As soon as their mouths collided, the kiss became charged with an unbearable wanting. Perhaps he could have kept the embrace from going too far if she hadn't responded so generously. But the instant her arms tightened around his neck and she tilted her head to give him better access, he lost every semblance of control. His mouth hardened over hers, hungry and demanding, determined to take all she had to offer. With a barely audible sigh, she opened to him, her utter trust and vulnerability as arousing as it was humbling.

He thrust his fingers deep into her hair, dislodging the scrap of gold net. Her waist-length hair tumbled downward and he caught the molten curls, but they were too vibrant to contain. Her hair overflowed, spilling across his arms. The texture felt soft as pillow down and yet ignited a sensation that lapped across his skin like wildfire. It scorched the nerve endings and sparked the explosive need to make her his by any means possible. She was a woman who resisted caging. But that didn't stop him from trying. He urged her further into his arms, enclosing her in a trap of muscle and sinew. She could escape with a single word, but he was determined she wouldn't have the chance—or the desire—to utter it.

His tongue mated with hers, teasing and tempting, eliciting a response as uninhibited as it was honest. Here was one aspect of her personality where control was futile, though he suspected she'd never realized that before. He could only hope the pleasure she experienced eased the shock of learning that such raw, primal urges decimated her reserve beyond any chance of recovery.

Feathers fluttered helplessly beneath his determined siege and he cupped her breasts through the thin silken barrier, absorbing her tremors of desire. For an instant, he felt her surrender, the pliant gifting of herself as she leaned into him, her spine bending backward in a graceful arch. There was a softness to her, an acquiescence as her body readied itself to accommodate stronger, harder angles. But most telling of all was the underlying tension that consumed her, the urgent, irrepressible desire to match him thrust for thrust, to surge toward a heightening of their desperate need until they reached a completion of emotions held too long in check.

They'd reached a crossroads. And as though suddenly realizing it, she curbed her reaction, gathering inwards. "What am I doing?" she whispered.

She turned her head aside, her posture painfully stiff, the breath shivering in her lungs. Tension radiated from her, a far different sort than before—disbelief and, possibly, regret. But at least she didn't rip free of his embrace. If anything, she clung to him as if he were the only steadfast object in a world gone badly awry. Whether she knew it or not, she instinctively trusted him. It gave him hope as he provided her momentary anchorage.

Finally she turned to look at him, her eyes as huge and dark and unreachable as the night sky overhead. "I don't want to be seduced."

"What a shame." Ever so gently, he swept errant curls from her face. Picking up the scarf he'd used for a mask, he secured her hair at the nape of her neck, knowing it would help restore her sense of control. "I suspect I could do it very well—at least with you."

Her laughter trembled with nervous strain. "Why doesn't that surprise me?"

"Would it help if I promised to be thorough?" he asked gravely. "Granted, it would take a lot of time." A lifetime, if he were lucky. "But I'd be happy to make the sacrifice." She moistened her lips with the tip of her tongue and he almost took the plunge again, dipping into that sweet interior and urging her toward an inescapable destiny.

"Hanna," he warned.

The harsh, bitten-off sound of her name caused an instant reaction. Carefully, she disengaged herself from his arms, putting the distance of the bench between them. "What about you?" She fought to regain her poise by returning to the mundane. "I've told you about myself, but I don't know anything about your life."

He couldn't think after that kiss they'd exchanged, could barely speak. And she wanted to discuss his history? Couldn't she tell? Didn't she sense how he felt? He smoldered with the need to take her in his arms again. It pounded in his blood and raced through his veins, simmering with every breath he drew. Did she have any idea? She couldn't. Or she wouldn't be staring at him so calmly. She'd be fleeing toward safety. Of course, he'd be incited to give chase, so perhaps she was wise to remain seated on the bench.

''We have plenty of time to learn about each other,'' he finally said.

''I'm in control, remember?'' Her mouth curved upward with more than a hint of wry humor. ''At least, that's what you keep telling me.''

He gritted his teeth as he fought to contain a desire that had gotten seriously out of hand. ''What do you want to know?'' he asked, giving in to the inevitable.

''Do you have family?''

''I'm one of six brothers.'' Just remembering his family helped bank the fire. They weren't going to be pleased when they discovered that he'd gone back on his word. Too bad. He wanted Hanna, wanted her more than he had any woman he'd ever known. And he'd known quite a few. Yet, not one of them had stirred him to act so impulsively.

"Six!" It took her a moment to digest that. "What are their names?"

"You don't believe me?"

"Come on. Tell me their names."

"Luciano is the oldest. Luc's married to Grace. Then there's the moodiest of the lot, Alessandro, followed by me, Stefano and Rocco. And bringing up the rear is Pietro. Satisfied?"

"Your mother didn't have any daughters? Did she mind?"

"If so, she never let on." He shrugged. "It's too bad, if you ask me. We would have enjoyed having a little sister to spoil."

"Yes, I imagine you would," she murmured drily.

He lifted an eyebrow. "What makes you say that?"

"You just seem the type."

"I trust it's a good type?"

To his amusement, she ducked her head. If it weren't so dark, he'd probably have seen her blush. "Yes," she muttered. "It's a very good type."

"Did you have brothers who spoiled you?"

"We were discussing your background, remember?" He didn't respond and she sighed. "For supposedly being in control, I don't seem to be getting my way very often. No, I didn't have any brothers or sisters. Satisfied?"

"Satisfied and sorry. You strike me as a woman in desperate need of some spoiling."

Her jaw tightened. "I was spoiled plenty growing up. If you ask me, it's an unnecessary indulgence."

"You think so?" An inexplicable anger raced through him, one he fought to keep well hidden. An indulgence? If ever there was a woman crying for a bit of spoiling, it was this one. More than anything, he wanted to ease her tension, to transform her frowns into laughter. To prove to her that intimacy wasn't to be feared and love not a miracle, but a given. "Time will tell. What other questions do you have?"

"Where do you live?"

"San Francisco. And you?"

"Maryland on the Delmarva Peninsula. It's a little town called Hidden Harbor." Her brows drew together again and it struck him that she was a woman who frowned more often than she smiled. He'd change that, too, and soon. "I never thought to ask.... Are you willing to relocate? What do you do in San Francisco?"

"I make my living seducing people." He smiled, catching the trailing ends of the scarf confining her hair and urging her closer. Leaning forward so his mouth was mere inches from hers, he asked, "I'm very good at it, wouldn't you say?"

"Very." She swallowed, staring at him in apprehension. It would appear he'd shaken her composure, something he'd take pains to do as often as possible since it helped her unfurl ever so slightly. "How... What..."

"How do I seduce people and what do I seduce away from them?" At her nod, he leaned closer still, his breath stirring the curls at her temples. "What I seduce from them is money. As much as they'll give me. How I do it is by being charming and sincere and very, very honest."

"You take their money?"

"Every cent. In return for services rendered, of course."

"Services…?" Her eyes widened in alarm and she attempted to pull free. "You mean you're a…"

"Salesman." He sighed. "Sad, but true."

Laughter broke from her, light and startled and delightfully unfettered. It was possibly the sweetest sound he'd ever heard. "I thought—"

"That I was a gigolo?"

"Yes."

"Disappointed?"

"A little." Her smile eased the blackness of the night. "Of course, if you were a gigolo, I wouldn't marry you."

"Ah… But if I were a gigolo, I wouldn't admit it. I'd sweep you off your feet and get my ring on your finger as quickly as possible."

"Aren't you forgetting a step? First, you'd have to determine I was worth marrying."

His amusement fled. "You're worth it, *carissima.*"

"How would you know?" She set her chin at an aggressive angle. "I don't wear my bankbook around my neck. I could be a pauper."

"I'm not talking about finances, so stop trying to put words in my mouth." He eyed her shrewdly. "But you're not ready to admit that, are you? I suspect you want to find a flaw somewhere. Are you looking for an excuse to leave the Cinderella Ball without a husband?''

''I want to marry. I'm just not certain I'll find the man here.''

''Or love?''

''Unnecessary.'' The word rasped through the soft night air, taut with defiance. ''Life's a balance sheet. In the end, balance the good with the bad and hope for the best. If you're lucky you'll stay in the black. If you're very lucky you get an extra perk or two.''

He cocked an eyebrow. ''Love being an extra perk?'' he asked in disbelief.

''Yes.''

Blunt and to the point, and possibly, the most telling comment of all. ''What about the men your family hoped you might marry? What was wrong with them?''

''Nothing,'' she admitted. ''They just weren't...right.''

''They left you with a zero balance?''

She flinched at having her words turned back on her. ''Something like that.''

Or was it that she didn't love them? She might deny the emotion, but he suspected that deep down it might be the one ingredient she wanted most of all. If he were any judge of the situation, his swan princess had never been deeply touched by that particular emotion. And as much as she wanted it, she also feared it. Perhaps he could help allay those fears. "And what about me? Do you think I might be right?"

He saw the caution darken her eyes, but her body swayed closer, seeming of its own accord. "How can I be certain?"

"You can't." He offered her an alternative to her balance sheet theory. "You can only go with what your senses tell you. You need to listen to your gut instincts. What do they say?"

"I don't think I was given gut instincts."

"Sure you were. Or you wouldn't have refused the men your family encouraged you to marry. You would have settled for a zero balance."

She tilted her head to one side, studying him. "Somehow, I doubt my family would approve of you. You're not logical. And you're far too handsome and charming."

"Thank you. I'll take their disapproval as a compliment."

"Doesn't that worry you...that my family might not like you?"

"Not at all. It will be my pleasure to change their opinion."

"I almost forgot." Amusement lurked in her eyes. "The great seducer, right?"

He cupped her cheek, sliding his thumb along the silken curve. "Have I seduced you into marrying me?"

"Yes." Whisper-soft, but adamant. That pleased him.

"Then they'll accept me, too."

"And if they don't?"

He gave an exaggerated sigh. "If I can't charm them, I'm afraid I'll simply have to beat them into submission."

She laughed again, the sound tainted with irony this time. "That will be interesting to see."

"So are we decided? Do we go find a priest or minister or judge?"

For a long moment, she continued to stare at him, as though she were searching those nonexistent instincts for an answer. Slowly, she nodded. "Just one last question."

"Fire away."

''What happens if it doesn't work out between us? Could we...could we try a trial run first?''

He didn't like the sound of that. ''A trial run?''

''Like...like a business contract. Could we try the marriage for a few months and see if it's working? If not, we go our separate ways, no hard feelings.''

No hard feelings? If he lost her, hard feelings would be the least of it. It was his turn to scrutinize her. It didn't take much to pinpoint the underlying nervousness, the hint of fear and bravado in the face of intense apprehension. ''Why are you really doing this, Hanna? If you're not sure about getting married, why go through with it?''

''I am sure.''

She was lying, but whether it was intentional or not, he couldn't quite tell. ''We can reassess our situation after a bit, if that would make you more comfortable.'' Though he'd do everything within his power to turn their trial-run marriage into a permanent union. ''How long is this probation period supposed to last?''

"Why don't we give it until the first of the year. That's what...? Sixty-four days."

His brows drew together. "You know how many days it is until the end of the year?"

"I'm a great believer in accurate timekeeping." She dismissed his comment with a wave of her hand and returned to the point. "If either party wants out by then, we'll go our separate ways. Agreed?"

He inclined his head, unwilling to commit aloud to something so alien to his basic nature. She might go her separate way, but once he'd made his vows, he fully intended to stick to them, come hell or high water. "So what happens next? Do we marry?"

"They told me when I arrived that there's a county clerk in the library. We're supposed to go there first and fill in a marriage application. After that, we have a choice of ceremonies. I believe they're upstairs off the ballroom."

Marc stood and offered his hand. "The library it is."

To his amusement, her apprehension had evaporated. Without a moment's hesitation, she slipped her hand in his. "Hanna Salvatore.

Sounds better than Hanna Tyler, don't you think?''

''Much better,'' he confirmed. ''In fact, it sounds perfect.''

CHAPTER THREE

DORA SCOTT, COUNTY CLERK...Marriage Applications Processed Here. Form a line, no cutting, no excuses and feed at your own risk.

Hanna exchanged an amused glance with Marc as they read the large sign on the library desk. "I wonder what that part at the end means," she murmured.

"It means," Dora interrupted, "that last time I did this gig, I put on ten pounds because people kept forcing hors d'oeuvres on me. Don't know why. But being the polite, kind soul I am, I ate every blasted one of 'em and then had to work my butt off for the next month to get rid of the less-than-polite results."

"So you'd rather we didn't feed you?" Marc asked.

"Didn't say that. Did you hear me say that? I said I ended up having to work it off."

"Got it." Marc turned to a nearby footman. "A tray of your best hors d'oeuvres, please."

"Oh, heaven help me, I'm not sure I can," Dora protested with a groan. The next instant, she offered a sly grin. "Aw, heck. Guess one little ol' tray won't hurt."

"We were told we could fill out a marriage application here," Hanna said, deciding it was time to get down to business. If she didn't hurry and get this over with, she might do something incredibly smart...like turn tail and run.

"Right you are. And since you caught me in a generous—not to mention hungry—mood, I'll get you processed pronto." She slapped forms in front of them just as the footman returned bearing a heavily laden tray. "Go to it folks, while I have myself a little snack."

Hanna picked up one of the pens lined up on the desk and tackled the application. It wasn't terribly complicated. Name, age, marital status. The only part that slowed her down came at the end. She glanced at Marc from the corner of her eyes. It would seem they were about to face their first little hurdle. How would a man with such strong family ties react? As she half expected, he paused in the middle of his scribbling and peered over her shoulder.

"It's not a test, you know," she dead-panned. "You can't get the correct answers by looking at my paper."

"That's what you think. This is the sort of information men commit to memory...if they're smart." He tapped the line that read date-of-birth. "Particularly this one and one other that I guess will show up on the certificate."

"What's that?"

"The date we married."

"Oh, right." She checked the bold-faced analog watch encircling her wrist. "It's twelve-oh-four. So it's officially tomorrow. Does that help?"

His soft chuckle ignited a chain reaction that started deep in the pit of her stomach before spreading outward in hot, sweeping waves. A reaction, moreover, she seemed helpless to control. "Tomorrow, huh? It'll be nice to have a wife so time-oriented. It should give balance to the relationship." He glanced at her form again. "Hanna Louise, huh? Pretty."

She returned the favor, checking his document, as well. "Marco? I think I like that even better than Marc."

Had she really admitted that? Judging by the unmistakable warmth filling his rich brown eyes, she'd not only said it, but with that one simple declaration, she'd given him immense pleasure. Such a simple thing. Just words. And yet, judging by his reaction, they'd been as meaningful to him as anything she'd ever done for the town of Hidden Harbor.

"My family often calls me Marco. So if you prefer that version of my name, feel free to use it."

"Thanks."

He resumed his examination of her application. "You didn't mention you were a widow."

"Didn't I?"

"I'm sorry, *carissima*. That's a rough one."

She stilled at the Italian endearment. "Are you doing your swashbuckler routine again?"

"No!" He gripped her shoulders and turned her to face him. Could salesmen fake sincerity? she couldn't help but wonder. Perhaps, but not like this. The compassion darkening

Marco's eyes and lining his face weren't put there in a glib attempt to impress her. His regret was sincere. "No. I wouldn't do that to you. I'm truly sorry. No one should have to face that sort of tragedy at so young an age. I remember how my father was after my mother died. If he hadn't needed to take care of the six of us, I doubt he'd be here, today."

It was her turn to offer compassion. "Oh, Marco. How terrible for all of you. How old were you when she died?"

"Eight."

There was a wealth of emotion in that one, simple word. She could hear the pain reflected in his voice and knew the death of his mother had had a profound effect on him. As profound an effect as her background had on her? It would appear they were more attuned than she'd thought. She reached out and covered his hand with hers. "I'm so sorry, Marco."

"You folks about done over there?" Dora interrupted.

Hanna glanced over her shoulder, wishing they had more time to discuss their respective pasts. But soon, they'd have all the time they needed. Perhaps too much, considering some of the details she'd kept from him. "We'll be through in another minute."

Leaning over the form, she diligently filled in the rest of the boxes...at least the boxes she could. Snatching up the document before Marco could peek again, she carried it to the desk, praying Dora wouldn't comment. To her relief, aside from an upswept eyebrow, the clerk didn't utter a word. Not the usual platitudes, not a smirk, not even a pitying look. Instead, she reluctantly set aside her tray of hors d'oeuvres and whipped through the processing of their forms.

"Now, show me some form of legal identification that says you are who you claim to be and we're set." Once that was accomplished she handed them a blue-and-white envelope. "Marriages are conducted in the salons off the ballroom. You give the papers in the envelope to whomever officiates. Got it? You'll receive a pretty certificate in return once the deed is done, but that one's for show. You'll get a certified copy in the mail in a couple weeks. Any questions?"

"I think that covers it," Marco said.

"Great. All that's left is to wish you folks good luck. But most importantly... Be happy." She reached for a cracker heaped with salmon. "Off you go before I get weepy. That always happens when I'm hungry."

Marco released another of his husky laughs—the one guaranteed to seduce a woman regardless of age or marital status. "Thank you, Dora. We appreciate your help." Dropping an arm around Hanna's shoulders, he swept her through the library door.

It took them a few minutes to make their way upstairs. The ballroom seemed to have grown since she'd last been there, the floor stretching before them like an endless ocean. As they charted a course across the expanse, she half expected one of the men gathered around her earlier to approach and demand an explanation for her disappearance. But none did. To her relief, they seemed to have found new love interests. By the time she and Marco were partially across the room, it felt as though the room hadn't grown at all, but had shrunk, and they were moving at lightning fast speed, so fast she could scarcely catch her breath.

Outside the salons, she froze, panicking. "Marco—"

His understanding was instantaneous. "It'll work out, Hanna. I promise."

"Maybe we're rushing into this." She turned blindly toward him. "Maybe we should wait."

"Do you want to return home, alone and unwed? Or would you rather go back together, as husband and wife?"

He'd played an ace card she didn't realize he possessed. Return to life as it had been? Caring for her family. Caring for the business. Carrying the burden of so many on her shoulders. Alone and unwed, said it all. Or she could have... *Marco.* Hanna shook her head. "I don't want to go home without you. But I don't know if this is right, either."

He caught her shoulders in his hands. "It is right," he insisted with quiet conviction. "I know it's hard for you to open yourself to another. But I won't hurt you, I swear it. Marry me, Hanna."

She stared at him, seeing only a stranger in her panic. But then her vision cleared and she saw, truly saw, the man standing before her.

At a little over six foot, Marco Salvatore wasn't the tallest man she'd ever met, not compared to the Tyler clan. But he had to be the most stalwart. Something about him spoke of indomitable strength, of a man not easily swayed by others. He regarded her steadily, his eyes—those wonderful, warm, coffee-brown eyes—were calm and direct and unwavering. No question, he was one of the best-looking men she'd ever seen.

And that gave her pause.

Marco Salvatore was a charmer, no two ways about it, precisely the sort of man Pru had warned her to avoid. People listened to his deep, rich voice, with the echo of his Italian heritage still lingering in the lilting tones, and they responded. They were helpless to resist. Between the pull of that voice, the sincerity of his gaze and the striking planes of his face— not to mention the lean elegance of his frame—he was a man who could charm a woman into giving up everything. With one softly spoken word, she'd turn her heart over to his keeping—her heart, her body, even her soul. But there was one aspect that frightened her more than anything else.

He was a man she could truly love. And love had no business in her life.

All the while she stood there and stared, he remained quiet and steadfast beneath her gaze. He didn't shift nervously as some she knew, or break into hasty speech. Nor did he give any sign of impatience. He simply waited and let her look her fill.

"Marc..." She'd reverted to the Americanized version of his name, perhaps as a subconscious effort to put some distance between them. "Maybe this is a mistake."

"Marry me, Hanna. Please."

Four simple words. But they said so much. More than any man ever had before. *Do it!* a part of her urged. She'd never have another opportunity like this, one that combined someone she found absolutely irresistible with a man who seemed to find her just as appealing. Her family couldn't interfere, her background remained shrouded in secrecy, at least for the moment. And he wanted *her*. She couldn't mistake the look in his eyes any more than she could mistake the passionate desire inherent in his kisses.

She took a deep breath. "Yes, Marco," she said, hardly believing that she, of all people, would take such a foolish risk. "I'll marry you."

"Civil ceremony or religious?"

"Civil."

He inclined his head, though she sensed he regretted her choice. "That would be this room, here." He opened the door to the nearest salon and gestured for her to enter.

She hesitated in the doorway, under-whelmed by what she saw. Oh, sure, the room was as elegant and beautifully furnished as everything else about this desert castle. But the ice-blue decor lacked something. It had a barrenness that chilled her, the formality and soullessness something that struck an all-too-familiar chord.

"Could we try another room?" she asked.

A tender smile transformed his face, sweeping across the chiseled features and making him even more attractive, if such a feat were possible. "My pleasure."

He opened the door to the next salon which offered a religious ceremony, and Hanna didn't hesitate, but stepped inside. If she didn't know better, she'd swear someone had reached inside her heart and pulled from it her most secret and childish longing.

It wasn't that the room was the most beautiful she'd ever seen, or the most elegant. But as sure as she stood there, it had to be the most homelike. Everything about it felt warm and welcoming, as if the room held its breath in anticipation of a noisy family erupting through the doorway at any moment. Brightly colored throw pillows were scattered about, heaped on the couch and tossed in front of a crackling fire. Fresh flowers of every hue and variety were stuck in earthen vases, along with cattails and wheat stalks and meandering vines. For the first time in her entire life, Hanna felt like she belonged.

An elderly gentlemen garbed in white robes stood at one end of the room, behind a low podium. He gave them a moment to look around. ''Do you wish to be wed?'' he asked.

Hanna nodded and he motioned them toward a pair of low stools placed in front of his podium. Marco took her hand, leading her to the stools, and handed over the packet of papers Dora had prepared. Without hesitation, he knelt and she followed suit.

"Before we begin, I'm required to ask that you give careful consideration to the step you're about to take," the clergyman explained. "Marriage is a serious commitment, not to be entered into lightly. So I ask that you face each other and study your partner carefully. Make sure that your choice is the right one."

Once again, Hanna turned and looked at Marco. And once again, he returned her gaze with a steadfast certainty that instantly expelled all doubt. She wasn't sure where this path would lead. That was unusual enough since she never walked down an unfamiliar road—or at least, one she hadn't carefully mapped beforehand. But somehow she knew that with Marco beside her she'd be safe. He wouldn't steal her precious control, nor would he force her to take a path she didn't want. He'd simply walk with her, making the journey a special one.

"I'm certain." The words seemed to be drawn from deep inside, uttered without hesitation and without conscious thought.

"You won't be sorry, *amor mio*." He turned to the official as though there'd never been a moment's question on his part. "Please begin."

"Very good. Join hands, if you will."

The words that followed washed over Hanna, spoken sometimes in English and at times in Latin, the soft sounds lingering in the air like a sweet fragrance. When it was her turn to speak the vows, she turned to Marco in silent panic. He squeezed her hands reassuringly and the words flowed, free and certain. And then he made his promises to her, promises to honor and cherish, to love and protect. Promises she knew he would try to keep because he was an honorable man—promises he didn't have a hope of fulfilling.

"Before I pronounce you man and wife, would you care to exchange rings? We have them on hand," the clergyman offered. "They're tokens, really. Just something to use until you can replace them with the genuine article."

"That's not necessary." Reaching into a special pocket she'd sewn into her costume,

Hanna removed a set of rings. "I brought these in case."

Marco took the gold bands from her, examining them carefully. "They're unusual. A family heirloom?"

"No." She sounded abrupt and knew it. But his question had hit an exposed nerve. "No, I found them in an antique shop not far from here."

"You know…" He held them up, squinting when they fractured the light, shimmering as though alive. "They almost look like they were made from tickets from the Cinderella Ball. See the scroll marks etched into the gold?"

The uncanny similarity had been precisely what had prompted her to purchase them. "The old woman who sold them swore they'd bring me luck." She shrugged, loath to admit to such superstitious nonsense. "Assuming I believed in such a thing."

"Which you don't," Marco guessed shrewdly.

Hanna shook her head. The shop owner had also claimed they would guarantee a happy and everlasting marriage. And like the most desperate and gullible of women, she'd handed over her credit card without even bothering to haggle over the price and bought the two rings. Who'd have thought that she, Hanna Tyler, could be accused of possessing a romantic streak? If the citizens of Hidden Harbor heard what she'd done, they'd laugh themselves silly.

Without a word, Marco took the smaller of the two rings and slid it onto her finger. It fit as though made for her. He lifted her hand and kissed it with all the charm and grace of a six-teenth-century courtier. ''Thank you for choosing these for us.''

He offered her the larger ring and with a bit less grace than he'd displayed, she thrust it onto his finger. It hugged his finger a bit more snugly than hers had. For some reason that pleased her. ''You're going to have trouble getting it off,'' she informed him with a shameful amount of satisfaction.

''Since I don't plan to take it off, that won't be a problem,'' he replied.

Her satisfaction turned to alarm. ''But what if—'' Glancing at the clergyman, she bit back her question. *But what if the marriage doesn't work out?* she'd almost said. Somehow that didn't seem like an appropriate question when they'd been wed for all of two seconds. "You won't forget our arrangement?" she asked instead.

"I haven't forgotten anything. I've made you promises and I intend to keep them. Every one of them."

Before she could question precisely what he meant, the clergyman interrupted. "Now that you've exchanged rings, it's my pleasure to pronounce you man and wife. Marco, you may kiss your bride, thereby welcoming Hanna Salvatore into your heart and into your life."

Hanna Salvatore. The name sounded as foreign as the ring on her finger. Not that that stopped her from lifting her face to her husband's or from accepting his kiss. Accepting? Why bother kidding herself? She lost herself in the blissful joining of their mouths, in the lush taste and scent of him. She could get used to this. Dear heaven, she could get used to this quite easily.

Promises, he'd said. In the plural. He'd promised before the ceremony to give their marriage a trial run. How in the world would she handle it, if he kept that part of their bargain? How indeed, since a temporary marriage was an all-too-likely possibility—one, in fact, that she'd insisted upon? The thought nearly shattered her. But then she remembered... remembered that he'd also promised during the ceremony to take her for his wife from this day forward. Maybe, just maybe, he'd keep that promise, instead. The thought filled her with a dangerous hope, warned that she'd already begun to care for this man.

Staring up at her brand-new husband, the taste of him still fresh on her lips, Hanna Salvatore realized she was in deep, deep trouble.

"Here we are," Hanna said, hoping to cover her nervousness with the cool, dispassionate announcement. They paused at the hotel door and she gestured awkwardly. "Would you like to come in?"

"For a little while," Marco agreed.

She hesitated, not quite sure what to make of that. A little while meant not all night. So, if he wasn't planning to spend the night, what precisely, did he plan? A quick tumble before

he left, just to consummate their new relationship? She shrank from the thought. What in
the world had she been thinking to marry a
complete stranger? How could she have taken
such a drastic step? Here she stood in the doorway outside her hotel room with a man she'd
only known for a few scant hours. He was her
husband, a man she'd committed to for the
next few months, a man she'd given every
right to…to… *To come in for a quick tumble
before he left!*

The key card fell from her nerveless fingers.

''Here, let me get that for you.''

He bent and picked up the slip of plastic,
inserting it into the locking mechanism while
she watched helplessly. No hesitation, no fumbling, no awkwardness. As though to acknowl-
edge his proficiency, the tiny light flashed
gaily from red to green. *Come on, you stupid
lock! Turn red again and get me out of this!*
she wanted to scream. Instead the lock gave
way with a loud clicking noise that retorted
down the hallway like a gunshot. She flinched,
not that Marco noticed. Twisting the knob, he
shoved the door open and gestured for her to
precede him into the one place she least

wanted to be with her brand-new husband—a bedroom.

Hanna hastened inside before he could think of doing something incredibly gallant and Marco-like, such as carry her over the threshold. Behind her the door slammed shut and she spun around in a swirl of feathers and ivory skirts. As though in a symbolic gesture, the scarf restraining her hair loosened and drifted to the floor with a silken sigh. Fiery curls spilled across her shoulders to her waist and she had an unnerving image of a red cape teasing the life out of a snorting, drooling, raging bull. She'd seen cartoons. She knew what the bull would do when provoked like that. She braced herself for impact.

The bull lifted a dark eyebrow. ''Something wrong?'' he asked mildly.

''Yes. No.'' She gestured awkwardly. ''My hair.''

''It's beautiful.''

''It came loose.''

''Yes, I see that.''

''I...I wasn't sure what you'd do.''

''Ah. That certainly fails to clarify matters.'' He approached and she steeled herself once

more. Circling her, he bent and plucked the
scarf from the floor, the scrap of silk trailing
from his hand like a whip. ''I believe you
dropped this.''

''It...it fell out.''

He snapped the wrinkles from it with a swift
flick of his wrist and she stilled, her breathing
shallow and rough. ''What would you like?''
he asked, coming up behind her. He draped the
cool black silk over her bare shoulders, dragging it across her heated skin, the scarf stirring
a reaction as potent as a lover's caress.
''Would you like me to tie your hair back
again?''

''Yes.'' She cleared her throat. ''Absolutely.''

''Or is this what you wanted...?''

The scarf rippled a sinuous path to the floor
like a dark flag of surrender. Wrapping an arm
around her waist, he urged her a single step
toward him, locking them together, spine to
chest. Whispering an Italian word rich with
passion, he swept her hair over her shoulder.
It flowed in a tidal wave of molten fire across
her breasts to her waist. He leaned into her,
the warmth of his breath stirring the fine curls

at her temple, his mouth so close to her cheek, she shivered beneath the promised impact. He pressed her closer still, melding their bodies.

''I don't think I want this,'' she whispered.

''You're nervous.''

Denying it would be pointless. ''Yes.''

''You're beginning to think you've make a terrible mistake.''

She sagged against him. Could the man read minds, as well? ''Let's just say that I'm having second thoughts.''

''All brides have them, or so I've been told.''

''Yes, but at least those brides have known their husbands longer than a few hours.''

''Not always. There are places where the bride and groom meet for the first time on their wedding day.''

She closed her eyes, laughter battling the most alien emotion of all—an overwhelming desire to give in to tears again. ''In case you're wondering, that doesn't make me any less nervous.''

''How do you suppose those couples made it through their first night together?''

"I suppose it depends on what sort of people they were. If...if the groom were a kind, understanding sort, he'd give his bride a chance to get used to marriage before... Before... You know."

"And if the groom wasn't a kind, understanding sort?"

She swallowed. "He'd force himself on her. After all, what choice would she have?" Turning in his arms, she clung to the front of his shirt. "But you're not that type of man."

He lifted an eyebrow, his expression frighteningly impassive. "No? You're so certain?"

"Yes!"

His eyes warmed, gentled. "Then why are you nervous?"

Just like that, her fear eased. She trusted him! She'd instinctively sensed he wouldn't do anything to hurt her. Perhaps she had gut instincts after all. Who'd have thought? She shrugged. "Call it an attack of nerves. It's awkward. We don't know each other well and married on impulse. I mean..." She attempted to smooth the creases she'd pressed into his shirt, ironing them along the hard, ridged contours beneath. But all that did was increase the intimacy of the moment and stir her anxiety to new heights. Her hand stilled, gathering the strong, steady beat of his heart within her palm. ''You told me your brothers' names, but I've tried and tried and I don't remember what they are. Silly, isn't it? I know there's six.''

''Five. Six sons, five brothers.''

''See?'' She tore free and began to pace, her hair billowing in agitated waves. ''I don't even have the number right. And then... There's your father. You haven't told me his name.''

''Papa.''

She stopped and stared at him, her brow wrinkled. ''What?''

''Just kidding, *carissima*. His name is Dom. But he'd be offended if you called him anything other than father or papa or dad.'' Marco folded his arms across his chest. ''What else?''

Hanna twisted her hands together. ''You said you were a salesman. But I don't know what you sell.''

''Does it matter?''

''How can you ask such a thing?'' she demanded. ''Of course it matters. When we go back to Hidden Harbor and I introduce you, guess the first question everyone will ask?''

"Let's see..." He pretended to frown. "What does he do for a living?"

She stabbed the air with her index finger. "Exactly! And I'll say... Why, he's a salesman. And they'll reply... Oh, really? What does he sell? And I'd have to say... Gee, I don't know." She lifted her hands in appeal. "Do you see where I'm going with this?"

"As frightening as it is to admit, yes."

"Right! It would look odd. So, anyway..." She fixed him with an inquiring stare. "What do you sell?"

"Anything and everything. I suppose it would be more accurate to say I put together products with vendors, money with those who need it. If someone has something they wish to sell, I find outlets for them."

That intrigued her. "You do?"

"I do."

She resumed her pacing. "See? That wasn't so difficult. I can explain that to people. I think we're on a roll here. Now what else?"

"How about your late husband?"

She faltered, aware the tables had just been given a sharp spin. "My...my husband?"

"Late husband. He is late, isn't he? I'm not going to arrive in Hidden Harbor and find him waiting for us, will I?"

"Er, no," she assured, hoping he wouldn't pick up on her evasiveness. "Not him."

"I can't tell you how relieved I am to hear that. So how long were you married?"

"Two months."

"Ah, sweetheart. I'm so sorry." His instant remorse made her feel worse than ever. "That must have been very difficult to lose your husband after so brief a marriage."

She couldn't deny it. They'd been two of the most difficult months she'd ever experienced. "He'd been ill for quite a while."

"And you married him, anyway?"

"Of course," she said simply.

"Did you love him?"

"I told you—"

"That's right. You don't believe in love, do you?"

"No." She set her chin and faced Marco squarely. It was one of those occasions when the truth hurt, when her resolution to hold emotion at bay seemed doomed to failure. "I...I cared for Henry. He was a dear friend."

"Interesting you'd marry the late Mr. Tyler considering you didn't love him." He tilted his head to one side. "Why would you do that?"

"It seemed the right choice at the time," she confessed. And it had. There hadn't been any other way to accomplish what she needed unless she'd married him. How odd that she'd put herself in the precise same situation again—marrying for need rather than more traditional reasons.

"Did he love you?"

Tears pricked her eyes and she bowed her head. "No," she whispered. "He respected me. He might have even liked me. But he loved his first wife."

"And you were willing to settle for that?" Marco asked incredulously.

"At the time it seemed…acceptable."

"And what about us?"

"What do you mean?" she asked evasively.

"Is what we have, what you hope we'll have in the future, just acceptable? Or is it more than that?"

An intense yearning caught her by surprise. It was a totally inappropriate emotion, but she couldn't deny its existence. She wanted more from this man than what she'd had from Henry. She wanted it with all her heart—the very heart she'd denied possessing. "I hope it'll be more."

His expression eased and she knew her answer had pleased him. "In that case, I have one final question for you."

Hanna eyed him warily. "What's that?"

"You asked for a trial marriage." A smile tilted his mouth. "When does it start?"

She braced herself once again. "Tonight. We can start the trial tonight."

CHAPTER FOUR

MARCO RELEASED HIS BREATH in a long sigh.
"I see. I guess I know what we should do."

"What?" Hanna asked, fighting for calm
and fast losing the battle.

He didn't take his eyes from her, but silently
approached. Good heavens, but he was graceful, moving with a fluidity that màde her wonder if he'd show that same supple skill in bed.
In bed! She froze, trapped between want and
apprehension, finding the knowledge that this
man could inspire such disparate emotions
downright frightening. No one should be able
to do that to her, certainly not a man she intended to share her life with. It would give him
too much power, not to mention far too much
control.

Marco lifted an eyebrow, halting inches
away. He stood so close she didn't doubt he
could hear the swift give and take of her
breath. "Nervous?"

There was no point in denying the obvious. "Yes."

"Don't be."

He cupped her shoulders and urged her into his arms. He smelled of sandalwood soap and some sort of bewitching cologne that should be legally banned from store shelves. The fragrance made her dizzy. Or was it Marco? She gazed into his eyes, seeing the gentle reassurance she'd sensed in him from their first meeting. Perhaps she wouldn't find this night so difficult. She could do it. It only involved a few more of those mind-blowing kisses. After that they'd get naked and tumble onto her bed together. He'd make love to her six or seven or twenty times and that would be it. All done, mission accomplished. Sure. She could handle that.

She groaned. Yeah, right!

Leaning down, he kissed her on the forehead. *"Buona notte, amor mio,"* he murmured.

It didn't take a mental giant to figure out what that meant. She didn't know whether to burst into hysterical tears or equally hysterical laughter. Instead, she retreated into a familiar air of detached calm, clinging to it with a ter-rifying desperation. "You're not staying, are you?"

"I don't think it would be best." He slipped a stray feather from her hair and pocketed it. "Not tonight."

For the first time in more years than she could recall, her poise threatened to desert her. She studied the wall over his shoulder, praying the bland surface would give her something to fixate on other than rich brown eyes and a charming smile. "Why?" she managed to ask. Could he hear the ache in her voice? Did those acute senses of his pick up on her bewilder-ment and confusion? Where had her precious control gone when she needed it most? Out the door, apparently, soon to be followed by her brand-new husband.

"Ah, *cara*. How can you ask that question while looking at me with such apprehension. You're not ready for this."

Her gaze flickered in his direction, then away. "I...I might be."

"No, sweet. I don't take unwilling women to my bed. Nor do I take sacrificial lambs."

"I'm not...unwilling."

"Nor are you willing."

He was right, though she hated to admit it. She gave in to the inevitable with a quick, regal nod. "If that's what you prefer."

"It's not what I—"

"Where are you going?" she cut him off, unable to handle much more without falling all over him in a disgusting, weepy mess.

"The Beaumonts are putting me up. I'll return to their place."

"The Beaumonts?" She remembered again seeing him standing near the reception line without a mask or costume. She'd never gotten around to asking him about that. "Are you a friend of theirs?"

"Not exactly. I'm staying at their invitation since my visit to their home coincided with the ball."

She steeled herself for the next question. "Will you be back?"

"First thing in the morning." He responded promptly, as if it weren't an unusual question for a new bride to ask her two-hour-old bridegroom. "You have my promise."

Relief threatened to turn her spine to summer-warmed tree sap and it took every ounce of control to remain upright. "And—and we'll go to Hidden Harbor?"

"Together, as husband and wife."

"You can stay tonight." She made the offer one last time, hoping against hope he'd take her up on it. "I won't make a fuss."

"No, I can't. Not without making you mine. And that's not going to happen until the timing is right." He pulled her close, his mouth pressed to the top of her head. "I'll see you in the morning, *moglie mia*."

She'd had a lot of practice shielding her emotions. This was no different from those others. So why did she find it so much harder? "I'm almost afraid to ask what you just said." If her comment was a final, desperate bid to get him to stay, it failed. Miserably.

He released her and crossed to the door, as though anxious to put as much distance between them as quickly as possible. Opening it, he glanced over his shoulder. "*Moglie mia.* It means, my wife."

And with that, he left. Left her whispering, "But I'm not your wife. Not really."

"Do you have any idea what the *hell* time it is?" Luc growled into the phone. "What is it with you Salvatores that you can't read a damned clock?''

Marc grinned. ''You're a Salvatore, too, unless I'm mistaken. And I can read a clock.''

''You just don't give a— Oh, sorry, sweetheart. Did I wake you?'' There was a murmured conversation and Luc said in an aggrieved voice, ''It wasn't me! It was Marc. He called because… I don't know why he called. Why the hell did you call, Marco?''

''To tell you that I'll be leaving Nevada later today.''

''And not a moment too soon! Did you get the Beaumont contract? You didn't do anything foolish, did you? You've had everyone worried sick that you'd come home with some gold-digging floozy on your arm. You're not going to do that, are you? What? Oh, sorry, sweetness. I didn't realize I was yelling.''

Marc sighed. The next few minutes weren't going to be pleasant. ''Yes, I got the contract.''

''Great. When will you be home?''

''I have a small stop first.''

''What small stop?'' Luc demanded suspiciously.

''Hidden Harbor, Maryland.''

"Never heard of it. What's in Hidden Harbor?"

"My wife's home."

"Your... *You better be joking, Marco!* What? Oh, sorry, *bellissima mia.* I didn't mean to shout again." He lowered his voice half a decibel. "You'd better be joking, little brother."

"It's no joke. Hanna and I were married last night. Maybe early this morning. I can't really recall." He held the receiver away from his ear and waited until the virulent stream of Italian slowed to a trickle. "No, I was not drinking. No, I have not lost my—you really shouldn't use language like that in front of your wife, Luc. She is a preacher's daughter—mind. No, she's not some sort of fortune hunter, although I suspect she hasn't a lot of money. And no, I'm not bringing her home for inspection. At least, not yet. I need time alone with her before I subject her to you hoodlums."

"What about Dom? What am I supposed to tell him?"

"Tell him I'm delayed on business."

"You want me to lie?" Luc asked, affronted. "To my own father?"

"Don't act like you've never done it before, big brother. I've watched you in action, remember?"

"That was different! I had a good reason."

"Well, so do I. Papa isn't a young man. I want to give the marriage a chance before springing it on him."

"You mean, you want to make sure it's going to last," Luc guessed shrewdly.

Marc's voice hardened. "It'll last. I've waited a long time for this woman. I'll do whatever it takes to make sure of it."

"If you're that certain, it must be my new sister-in-law who's having second thoughts. What? Oh, didn't I mention, precious? Marc got married. No, he hasn't asked to talk to you. I'll explain it later. No, sweetness, you don't need to tell him— Marc, it's for you."

"Marco, what have you done?"

"Hello, Grace. How's it going?"

"Terrible. Spill it, what have you done?"

"The same thing you and Luc did."

She sighed. "Yes, but couldn't you have learned from our mistakes? If you thought our marriage caused an uproar, it's nothing compared to what will happen when this gets out.''

''The only way it'll get out is if you or Luc do the outing.''

''Oh, right.'' She chuckled. ''So, what's she like? What's her name?''

''Her name's Hanna. She's beautiful. Intelligent. And furled.''

''Furled?''

''Cautious.''

''Oh, dear. No wonder you want to wait before introducing her to your family.''

''You got it. Do me a favor, will you, Grace? Try and keep Luc from pulling some crazy stunt...like showing up on Hanna's doorstep.'' At her snort, he sighed. ''Yeah, yeah. I know. It'll be a challenge. But try and keep him out of my hair for a few weeks, okay? Distract him. Tell him you're pregnant or something.''

''I am.''

It took a moment for that to sink in. ''You're *what?* Really? Are you serious? Have you told Luc?''

''Really. Very serious. And I will as soon as we hang up. Will that provide a good enough distraction?''

Marc laughed. "Yeah. That should do it. Congratulations, sweetheart. I know little Gina's been asking for a brother or sister."

"Mmm. So has Luc. And Alessandro, and Stefano and Rocco. Pietro and Carina have mentioned it a dozen or two times, as well. Not to mention Dom. Little did I realize when I married Luc that our love life would be orchestrated by the entire Salvatore clan."

"Which is precisely why I'd appreciate your giving Hanna and me some breathing space." He heard Luc's voice raised in the background and suspected Grace's news had just leaked. "Tell big brother congratulations and that I'll call in a few days. Take care of yourself."

"Good luck, Marc. I hope she knows what a wonderful husband she's gotten for herself."

"If she doesn't, I'm sure you'll be the first to tell her. *Ciao!*"

"*Ciao,*" she said with a laugh, and broke the connection.

For a long time, Marc sat and stared at the phone. In a few minutes, he'd thank his hosts for their generous hospitality and for signing a contract with the Salvatores—not to mention providing him with a bride—and depart. He'd catch a cab to the Grand Hotel and pick up his wife. It was the events that would follow which concerned him.

His darling wife had many admirable qualities. But there were a few that, quite frankly, worried him. For one thing, she wasn't being open with him, not about her background and not about her life in general. If she were broke or deep in debt, perhaps due to her late husband's illness, he could understand her reticence. But he knew it was more than that. He'd seen her completed marriage application, even though she'd tried to conceal if from him. Eventually they'd have to discuss a few of the more pertinent details.

Even that didn't matter. What did was her lack of trust, a problem he suspected would comprise the most difficult part of their marriage. Hanna was a fiercely independent woman, a quality he quite liked in a wife. It reminded him of his sister-in-law, Grace. There was only one small problem with that. A husband and wife needed to work together as a team. Compromise would be necessary at times. And on occasions, one would have to accede to the wishes of the other, trusting the partner to make the best decision. He suspected his dear wife would find that a particularly challenging skill to master.

Still… When he looked into Hanna's hazel eyes and saw the longing she tried so hard to hide… When he sensed the sweet emotions she fought to keep in check… When he tasted the desire filling each kiss… When he held her in his arms and felt the rightness of their joining, felt the trust and acceptance her body instinctively offered, he knew he'd made the only possible decision. This woman was his soul mate.

Now he had to convince his sweet wife of that fact.

He grinned. But he would. He had a lifetime to accomplish his goal.

The day went steadily downhill after he left the Beaumonts. The minute he arrived at The Grand Hotel, Marc realized he'd made a tactical error in not spending the night with his new bride. She'd already checked out of the hotel and sat in the lobby, her suitcase at her feet. If it hadn't been for the distinctive flash of auburn when she turned her head, he doubted he'd have recognized her.

She'd dressed in a navy suit, a color that did absolutely nothing for her, the stark white collar washing the natural vibrancy from her face. As though to defy nature, she'd slicked her hair back, screwing it into an excruciating knot at the nape of her neck, the style so stifling even the natural vibrance of the color had trouble escaping. And she'd perched plain black reading glasses on the tip of her nose, the frames secured around her neck with a thick cord.

Heaven protect him, he'd married a schoolmarm!

"Carissima," he greeted her uneasily, leaning down to offer a kiss. She turned her head at the last possible moment and his mouth collided with her cheek.

"You don't have to keep up the Don Juan act, remember?"

"Don Juan was Spanish. I'm of Italian descent." He straightened, his spine so stiff, it was a wonder it didn't crack in half. "I apologize if you find the endearments offensive, but that's how we were raised. I come from an affectionate family—affection we display openly, both in physical ways and through our words.''

She had the grace to blush, not that such a small show of remorse satisfied him. ''I guess I'm not used to it.''

''I can understand that.''

His eyes narrowed. There was another matter they needed to address and he cursed himself again for not spending the night with his bride, since this issue could have been dealt with in the privacy of their bedroom. More likely, it wouldn't have come up at all, since a night of intimacy would have resolved their current awkwardness.

''I can also understand your reluctance to greet your husband with a kiss while in public. If you are shy about such things, you have only to say so. But perhaps in future you'd be so kind as to say hello before criticizing me.''

Her blush intensified and she pressed her lips into a firm line—but not before he caught the betraying tremble. ''You're right. I shouldn't have said what I did.''

Gently he leaned down and plucked the glasses from the tip of her nose. Ah-ha. He could see the faint purple beneath her eyes. It would seem his wife hadn't gotten any more sleep than had he. "We're tired, *ca*—Hanna. We acted impulsively last night and it's understandable that we'd have second thoughts this morning, especially since we didn't spend the night together to solidify our marriage."

"That was your choice, not mine!" Her voice splintered on the final word and she fumbled for the glasses dangling from the end of the cord around her neck and thrust them back in place. But it was too late. He caught the diamond-bright glitter that could only come from tears.

"So it was," he conceded ruefully, crouching in front of her so they were on the same level. "A mistake I take full responsibility for. Come. Let's not snap at each other. Someone might get hurt. What do you say? Shall we start over?"

She gave a small nod, which was probably as much as could escape with her hair in such a tight twist. Marc stifled a sigh. He had a lot of ground to reclaim before he found his swan princess again.

"I ordered a cab," she said in what he sensed was her version of an olive branch. "And I reserved a ticket for you at the airport."

"Thank you. That was very thoughtful."

"I...I guess we'd better go."

He offered his hand and after the slightest of hesitations, she took it. Once again her dislike of public displays of affection was brought home to him and he couldn't help but wonder at the cause. But he noticed that despite that, her fingers clung, refusing to release him even when she could have gotten away with it. It was a small thing. But it was a start. Not only did she need him, but she wanted him. She simply didn't know how to let her guard down enough to ask.

Outside the hotel, she hesitated. "About those endearments," she said in a small rush. "I'm sorry about what I said. I really don't mind them."

"Are you sure?"

She offered one of the direct looks that were such a part of her nature. "Positive. I'm sorry I was rude. I'm...nervous."

"About going home?"

"Yes."

The cab pulled up and Marc loaded first his wife, then the luggage. Hanna didn't look nervous. If anything, she looked scared to death. He sighed. Today hadn't gotten off to a good start and no doubt it wouldn't improve any time soon. A fact, he suspected, that would be borne out over the next several hours.

"There are a few things I may have neglected to mention."

Marc glanced at Hanna. They were the first words she'd uttered since they'd left the small municipal airport outside Hidden Harbor. In fact, aside from telling the cab driver their destination, she hadn't managed a single syllable. So she was finally going to open up. About time. "A few things you neglected to mention," he repeated. "Let's see... Like about your parents?"

She stilled. "You saw?"

"On the marriage application? Yes. I assumed from your attitude last night that you didn't want to talk about it."

"I didn't. Don't."

He shrugged. "Fine. Tell me when you're ready."

"I was..." Her gaze flickered toward the cabbie and she lowered her voice. "Let's just say I didn't have a normal childhood. Not one like yours. The town is my family."

His eyebrows shot upward. "The entire town?"

"Yes. Every last blessed one."

Before he could ask any further questions, the taxi pulled up to the curb outside a large brick building that looked like it might have been a factory at some point. "What's this?" Marc asked, unable to ignore an intense feeling of foreboding.

"This is where I work." She thrust open the door and climbed from the cab. "Well, and where I live, too."

"This town—the one that's like a family— keeps you in a factory?" he asked with undisguised horror. He exited the taxi and paid off the driver, surprised when the man actually removed the luggage from the trunk and lined the pieces up on the sidewalk. Perhaps small towns were like that. It would make a welcome change.

"No one *keeps* me anywhere. This is where I choose to live." She smiled encouragingly. "It's quite nice inside. You'll see."

"Looks like a busy place."

"Yes...." She glanced at him, catching her lower lip between her teeth. "I think someone may have called ahead to warn people I was returning."

"Warn?"

"Maybe alert would be a better word."

"And why, *moglie mia,* would everyone need to be alerted?" He folded his arms across his chest. "A welcome party, perhaps?" For the first time she directed her gaze elsewhere. It was a telling action, and one that caught his attention as nothing else would have.

"No." She cleared her throat. "Not exactly."

"Then what exactly?"

"You were bound to find out sooner or later."

He fought to rein in his temper, silently cursing that he considered himself the "patient" Salvatore. Right now, he didn't feel the least patient. In fact, if he didn't get some answers soon, he'd display his anger to a degree that would have shocked Dom and his five brothers. "More secrets?"

"Not a good start?" she questioned with a lightness that failed to ring true.

"No."

"I'm sorry, Marco. Maybe it was your talk about being a gigolo. I know you're not. It's just…" She released her breath in a gusty sigh. "The truth is, I'm fairly good with money."

"Fairly good?"

"Okay, *very* good."

"And?"

"And all these people are here because they want to see me about various financial matters."

"You're a financial advisor?"

"If you go heavy on the advisor part, I guess that's as good a title as any."

The tightness building inside diminished and he managed to smile. "Is there a better title?"

"Queen. Or empress." A teasing expression sparkled in her gaze. "Take your pick."

"Cute." He liked it when she laughed. It emphasized the flashes of gold in her eyes and brightened her entire face. She was stunning like this. "I've never kissed a queen," he said, gathering her in his arms. "Or an empress. Welcome home, my lady."

He half expected her to stiffen and pull away. Instead, she relaxed against him, lifting her face to his. Carefully, he slipped his fingers into her hair, feeling the tight strands loosen and curl around his hands. Then he kissed her. He reveled in the generous sweetness of her mouth and the warm sigh that welcomed him home. Her hands clung to his shoulders as though they were all that kept her anchored to the ground. If they hadn't been standing outside her office building, he'd have swept her into his arms and found someplace private, someplace where he could offer the completion that should have been hers the night before. But that wasn't currently an option and he reluctantly released her.

"I'm sorry about last night."

"Sorry?" Her brow wrinkled. "Why are you sorry?"

"It's my fault our marriage got off to such a bad start. I should have stayed with you. That way we'd have awoken together on our first day as husband and wife."

An unmistakable yearning deepened the color of her eyes. ''Why didn't you?''

''I thought I'd give you time to get used to the idea of having a husband. Instead all I did was give you time to have second thoughts.'' Regret filled him. ''And you did have them, didn't you?''

''Yes.''

''You still have them.'' It wasn't a question.

She evaded a response with a noncommittal shrug. ''Why don't we go in now?''

''I'll do better tonight, I promise.''

She withdrew again, pulling inward to a place he couldn't reach. At least, not yet. ''I'd rather discuss this later.''

He gave in with good grace. ''Where should I put the luggage?''

''There's a small closet under the staircase. If you'd leave them there, I'd appreciate it. Then come on up and join the fray.''

He assumed from her request that she wanted a moment or two to warn her staff of his presence. Fair enough. He could understand her need for privacy. As soon as they entered the building, she pointed in the general direction of the closet. ''I'll be along in a few minutes,'' he assured. With a quick smile of agreement, she headed up a broad set of wrought-iron steps, giving him the opportunity to look around.

Hanna was right. The place did appear better on the inside than from the street. Though not by much. Desks, frantically working employees, ringing phones and a bustling environment comprised the first level of her factory cum office building. Despite that, the work zone struck him as sterile. Scattering some plants and rugs about wouldn't hurt. Hell, even some color would be an improvement. Perhaps after they'd been married a while he could offer some tactful suggestions using his family business, Salvatores, as an example.

Deciding he'd delayed long enough, he ascended the iron steps. The upper floor was clearly the executive level, the stairs opening onto a large reception area—a reception area jammed with people who were arguing at the top of their lungs. Ahh. Just like home.

Marc braced a shoulder against a convenient pillar and remained quiet, observing before acting, all the time wondering where the hell his darling wife had gotten to. He finally saw her in the very center of a circle of large male bodies, a fact that put him on instant alert. Considering the size of the men surrounding Hanna, he'd never have noticed her if it hadn't been for a distinctive flash of red.

"Don't listen to Janus, Hanna. My guy's better. Look at him." A beefy arm waved in the direction of a plush couch where a bodybuilder sat perched on the edge of an over-stuffed cushion. At least he tried to perch. Unfortunately, the couch wasn't designed for either perching or steroid-enhanced jocks. He kept sinking into the ticking and floundering awkwardly in the cushy depths.

"But, I don't need him," came Hanna's voice. It sounded a bit testy, not to mention muffled, perhaps from trying to work its way through such an impressive wall of brawn.

"You're full of it, Jeb," another of the men interrupted. "She doesn't want her muscles on the outside. She wants them on the inside. Kip is perfect for her." Another beefy arm—a different one—gestured in the opposite direction. Perched more successfully on the edge of a chair sat the human version of a praying mantis, his skinny arms and legs folded into awkward angles. "He's smart."

"Boys, you don't understand," Hanna tried again. "I've already found—"

"You're both wrong," came a third voice. "I got her one who's pretty and smart. Top that!"

Marc scanned the room, his gaze landing on the one he assumed must be Mr. Pretty-Smart. Blond, blue-eyed and solemn-faced, the man potentially had more than two brain cells functioning at the same time. The only remaining question was what the hell was going on around here. Who were these people and why were they busily offering a selection of men to his wife? Somehow he doubted it had anything to do with financial advice.

"Boys! I told you. I'm not interested in—"

"But, Hanna. You need a husband. We're just trying to help out."

It was all Marc had to hear. Straightening from his lounging position, he waded into the circle, neatly cutting an opening between the three giants and just as neatly extracting his wife.

"Hey!" one of them protested—Jeb perhaps. "What are you doing?"

"And you are?" Marc asked.

"Maybe I should introduce you," Hanna began nervously.

"Don't trouble yourself, *bellissima mia*. We're grown men. I'm sure we can straighten this out between us." He flexed his fist. At least, he certainly hoped to have that opportunity.

"What the hell did he say?" demanded another of Hanna's guards. "He called her a funny name! You want me to pound on him, Mother T?"

Mother T? "I called her beautiful," Marc was only too happy to explain. "It's an Italian term of endearment. It's one I often use when addressing *my wife*."

It took several minutes for that to sink in. Apparently their brain cells were as limited as the muscle-bound jock on the couch. Finally the information must have filtered along the underused path from their ears to their brains because the three men ringing his wife dropped identically squared-off jaws. They glanced first at Hanna who sighed, then at each other, exchanging narrow-eyed looks. Turning as one to glare at Marc, they said in unison, "Your *wife?*"

"Why yes," Marc confirmed. "I believe that's the correct term for the woman one marries." He turned to Hanna. "Do I have it wrong, my sweet? Sometimes my English, it's not so good."

"Cut the Zorro act, Marco. Your English is fine and you know it!"

"First Don Juan, now Zorro. Both fine Spaniards. But I, *cara,* come from solid Italian stock." He bared his teeth, laying on the accent good and strong. "So. If my English is good, that means I have my terms right. You're my wife and I'm your husband. That only leaves one question." He gestured toward the giants. "Who the *hell* are these *cafoni?*"

Hanna released another sigh. "I'm not even going to ask what that means, since I'd rather not have my office ripped apart once we hear the translation. But to answer your question, this is Jeb, Janus and Josie. They're…they're my sons."

CHAPTER FIVE

MARC TOOK A SPLIT SECOND to absorb what she'd said. "Your *sons?*" he repeated in patent disbelief.

"You tell him, Mother Tyler," the "sons" in question cheered from the sideline.

"Salvatore!" Marc didn't take his eyes off his wife, hoping to impress her with that fact as much as he impressed the three giants. "She's Hanna Salvatore now."

"Whatever. Want us to take him out back and explain it to him, seeing as his English is so bad and all?" Jeb-Janus-Josie offered.

She turned in a flash. "No! I do not want you to take him anywhere. I know I should have warned you—"

"Not to mention your husband," Marc inserted smoothly.

She winced. "All right, fine. Not to mention my husband. But I didn't expect everyone to be here waiting for me. Us."

Her explanation didn't appease him even a little. "And I didn't expect our welcoming party to consist of a line of potential husbands."

"Are you two really married?" one of her "sons" asked.

"We married last night." Her brow wrinkled. "Or maybe it was early this morning. I'm not sure."

For some odd reason her comment caused a full thirty seconds of silence. Strange and stranger. "You're not sure?" the middle one finally asked. *"You?"*

She gave an feigned apologetic shrug. "I wasn't really watching the clock."

That seemed to shock them even more. "You weren't watching?"

"No."

"Well, that tears it," the largest of the three growled. "Now we know it was a mistake. How about we give you a quickie divorce to match your quickie wedding? Or better yet, an annulment. Any chance that's still possible?"

Color flamed in Hanna's cheeks. "Jeb—"

That tore it! "Apologize. Now," Marc rapped out.

Jeb folded his arms across his massive chest and grinned. "You're kidding, right?"

"Not even a little."

"Tell you what. You can feel free to make me, if you're up to it. Otherwise—"

Before he could even finish what he'd been about to say, Marc had Jeb flat on his back, struggling for breath, the reverberation from his hitting the floor still echoing through the building. Marc planted a booted foot in the middle of Jeb's chest. "You were saying?"

"How the hell did you do that?" the smallest of the three asked. Josie perhaps.

He laid the accent on good and strong. "It's an Italian thing."

"Maybe I should go to school and learn me some Italian." He whistled in appreciation. "I never met anyone who could take down Jeb."

Marc smiled coldly. "Now you have." He returned his attention to the brother spread across the floor. "I believe you were about to offer your...*mother* an apology."

"Yeah, right." Looking both abashed and extremely uncomfortable, he said, "Sorry, Mother T. I didn't mean to insult you."

Hanna glanced at Marc with huge pleading eyes. Now why did she have to go and make him feel like a heel when it was his duty to protect her? He folded his arms across his chest and waited her out. It didn't take long.

Her attention switched to the Tylers. "I'm sorry, boys, I really am. I hate violence, you know that." She twisted her hands together. "But as much as I prefer calm, rational discussion over physical action—"

"In Jeb's case it flat-out doesn't work," the middle one finished for her. "He doesn't agree with anything unless it's bigger or stronger or harder than he is."

"I understand this comes as a shock, but you'll have to accept that I know what I'm doing." She eyed the other two boys. "That goes for all of you."

"Yes, ma'am," they said in unison.

She glanced at her husband. "Marco, please. Let him up now."

"Very well, my sweet."

He removed his foot and pivoted, wrapping an arm around Hanna's waist as part of the same swift maneuver. Before she could utter a single word of protest, he swept her toward a door he hoped led to her office. It would have been a damned shame if he'd ushered her into a closet. To his relief, he guessed right.

Once inside her office, he turned, blocking the doorway. "Just so it's clear," he addressed Hanna's family. "Hanna is no longer Mother T. She's now Signora Salvatore." And with that, he slammed the door and threw the lock. Not even the solid oak could keep the muffled sound of the ensuing argument from worming a path through the wood.

Hanna hesitated in the middle of the room and stared at her brand-new husband. This wasn't quite the homecoming she'd planned. For a long moment, he simply stood with his back to her, the muscles along his spine and shoulders corded with tension. Hanna watched as he collected himself before facing her. He smiled pleasantly enough, but she suspected beneath the surface he was flat-out furious. Perhaps if they'd been married longer, she'd know how to handle an irate husband. Unfortunately, she didn't. Her former husband had never lost his temper with her. Come to think of it, *no one* ever had.

Until now.

"I guess I should have mentioned the boys," she began, taking a hasty step backward.

"That might have been a good idea," he agreed, approaching.

To her disgust, she found herself continuing to retreat. This was becoming a habit, and a bad one. First last night, now today. "I wasn't quite sure how to broach the subject."

"How about... I married a man who had three sons, all of whom are at least five years older than me."

"I...I guess that was one way to have said it." She bolted behind her desk. "Although Josie and I are the same age."

"The one who wants to take Italian lessons?" he paused long enough to ask.

"Yes."

"Which means Papa T was substantially older than you."

"Do you always do that accent thing when you get upset?" Maybe one of these days she'd learn to keep her mouth shut. A frown settled on his brow and his eyes grew so dark, it reminded her of an angry storm blotting out the midday sky.

"Are you insulting me?" he asked very, very softly.

"No! You...you just start talking with a teeny-tiny bit of an accent every time you get upset." She pinched her fingers together to show him teeny-tiny. "I noticed it at the hotel this morning."

He inclined his head, his anger abating somewhat. "I suppose it's possible. Whenever we argue at home, we switch to Italian. My youngest brother, Pietro, often found himself at a disadvantage since his Italian was almost nonexistent. But it's improved immensely since he married Carina. Now he can yell with the best of us."

"Yell?" Hanna tried to swallow her nervousness. Not that it worked. She couldn't remember a time anyone had ever yelled at her. Or argued, for that matter. People tended to explain things to her—a lot and at great length. They always had. But raise their voice? Never. "I'm not sure I'd enjoy yelling."

"With hair like that?"

She folded her arms across her chest and glared. "Red hair does not mean a person has a temper. That's a stereotype. Like…like a dumb blonde.''

''You don't need to explain to me about stereotypes. I've had my fair share of experience with them.'' He cocked a sooty eyebrow. ''Are you done avoiding the discussion?''

''What discussion?'' Another bad question. Maybe she should try another tack. Before she could come up with one, he planted his hands on her desk and leaned toward her.

''The one where you tell me what the *hell* is going on around here.''

''Are you shouting?'' she demanded indignantly—and in as loud a voice.

''Damn right I am. You brought me here without giving any advance warning of what to expect.''

''I thought we'd have an opportunity to discuss it once we got—''

''No!'' He cut her off with a sweep of his hand. ''You waited because you were afraid I wouldn't come otherwise.'' Someone started pounding on the door and he swivelled to glare at it. ''Would you like me to handle that?''

After what he did to Jeb? Not a chance. ''I'll buzz through to my secretary's desk and ask what the problem is.''

"Your secretary?"

"She was out of the office when we arrived. Usually she's quite good at guarding the door, but for some reason today..." Hanna frowned in suspicion. "I wonder if they sent her off on a fool's errand so they'd have a chance to jump me?"

The level of pounding increased. Realizing that if she didn't do something about it, Marco would, Hanna went to the phone and buzzed Pru's desk. It was answered promptly, though not by her secretary. "Hanna?" a concerned male voice asked. "Are you all right? We thought we heard shouting."

"Yes, Janus. Everything's fine."

"Maybe we should come in and make sure."

Not a good idea. "I don't need you to come in. There's a few things I neglected to mention to Marco—"

"Like us?" It was Josie now. Apparently they'd found the speaker button.

"Yes, like you three."

"And Dad?" he asked shrewdly.

"That, too. So, if you'll all leave and take your latest offerings along with you, I'd ap-

preciate it.'' With luck they'd read ''offerings'' to mean the three suitors they'd dragged
in for her inspection.

There was a brief, low-voiced argument and
then, ''Not a chance,'' Jeb retorted. ''We're
staying right here until we know you're safe.''

Just great! She shot an uneasy glance toward
Marco, who was growing visibly more impatient by the minute. He crossed to a wall chart
that displayed her five-year goals and pretended to give it his full attention. Or perhaps
it really had captured his interest, since he
leaned closer to study something. ''I'll be fine
if you'll give me some time to discuss the situation with my husband.'' Although clearing
out the reception area would also help. Too
bad she couldn't convince Jeb of that. ''I'm
going to hang up now and I want the three of
you to be quiet.''

''If we hear any more shouting, we're coming in.''

''We won't shout.'' She gave her husband
a pointed look. Not that it did much good,
since he stood with his back to her. ''So you
won't need to come in. Jeb… I have to go. I'll

talk to you in a little bit.'' With that she hung up the phone.

''Now where were we?'' he asked, facing her.

''I believe we were working our way toward shouting in Italian. Fortunately for us both, I don't know any.'' She held up her hands in surrender. ''So you win.''

''Excellent.''

''And as a gracious winner, you'll now allow bygones to be bygones.''

''Ah. Is that how it works?''

She nodded, a tentative, conciliatory smile playing around her mouth. ''Absolutely.''

''Tell me something, Hanna. This wall chart...'' He gave it his full attention again. ''What is it?''

''My five-year plan. See?'' She pointed. ''It says so at the top.''

Humor gleamed in his eyes at her gentle teasing. ''You do that a lot? Plan things?''

Her entire life revolved around a schedule. It always had. ''Oh, I suppose I do have a tendency to plan,'' she conceded blithely. ''It helps keep me on track.''

To her dismay, he flipped to the page behind the one displayed on the wall. The one she preferred to keep hidden from prying eyes. Did those prying eyes include her husband's? Apparently, not. "And this page?" he asked, his voice reflecting an edge.

She stiffened, as she remembered precisely what was on that chart. "It's personal."

He studied the chart for an interminable minute. "Interesting." The top sheet dropped back into place with a soft whoosh and he turned to confront her. "You have goals for your personal life, as well as your business. And you say you only have a *tendency* to plan?"

She shrugged. "Blame it on my upbringing."

"I would except for one small problem."

"What's that?"

His smile held a dangerous quality. "You haven't bothered to tell me about your upbringing. In fact, you haven't bothered to share more than the bare-bone facts of your life. Including that you had a five-year plan to find a husband." He glanced toward the chart again and cocked an eyebrow. "Me, I assume?"

"You saw."

How could she doubt it? His reaction had been a clear enough indication. From the moment they'd met, Marco had been open and warm and affectionate—generous in both spirit and attitude. But from the second they'd arrived in Hidden Harbor a reserve had settled over him. Not that she could blame him. He'd had a lot to deal with since his arrival. And every bit of it was her fault for failing to be up front with him from the start.

"Why did you want to marry?" he rapped out. "Why is that an actual goal?"

"Tomorrow's my twenty-seventh birthday." Her explanation sounded ludicrous and they both knew it. But how could she make him understand everything that had led up to establishing those goals, both personal and professional?

"And?"

"And when I graduated from college, I formulated a five-year plan."

"One for business and one for your personal life?"

She nodded. "I knew I had this job waiting for me, that Mother Brent would train me to take over from her when she retired."

He studied the chart through narrowed eyes. ''That's not quite what this chart says.''

''That's because she died unexpectedly not long after I graduated. There was a lot for me to learn. It required a plan.''

''And this is your plan.'' She couldn't tell from his expression whether or not he approved. It shouldn't matter, but for some reason it did. ''That still doesn't explain your decision to marry at the end of five years.''

No it didn't. And having it stated so baldly made her feel foolish. ''I wanted to marry and have the business sorted out by the time I was twenty-seven.''

''Let me guess. Once you set yourself a goal—''

''I keep it.''

''And tomorrow is the five-year deadline?''

''Yes.''

''Isn't that a little extreme?'' he demanded. ''I can understand your hoping to marry before you're thirty or to have children within a certain time frame. But to actually go to a marriage ball in order to meet some schedule you set for yourself five years ago—'' He shook his head.

"That isn't the only reason I went."

"Do your..." He waved a hand toward the outer office. "Do the Tyler boys know about your goal to remarry? Is that why they have a line of potential husbands stretching from here to Baltimore?"

A smile flirted with her mouth. "It doesn't extend quite that long."

"You're avoiding the question."

"I've never told anyone other than Pru about my goal."

"Then why are they offering you men like a box full of chocolates?"

"Chocolates?" Her smile grew. "I think I might like chocolate better, though I can't remember the last time I had any."

To her relief, she'd succeeded in diverting his attention. "You can't remember? Good grief, woman. How's that possible?"

"I don't know. I was discouraged from eating it as a child and have never been particularly tempted as an adult."

"You've obviously been sadly deprived. I'll have to see what I can do about that." His expression hardened and she knew her brief respite from his questions was over. Too bad.

She'd hoped to escape relatively unscathed. "That still doesn't explain that nonsense in your reception area. Why are your former step-sons parading men in front of you like studs at an auction?"

She sighed. "Ever since their father died, the boys have been eager to see me remarry. I'm not quite sure why. Maybe it's their way of thanking me for caring for Henry while he was ill. Maybe they equate marriage with happiness."

"Don't you?" She remained stubbornly silent and anger flashed in his eyes. "Answer me, Hanna. Do you equate marriage with happiness?"

She folded her arms across her chest. "We discussed this last night, remember? I equate marriage with companionship. I suppose a by-product of companionship would be happiness." Her gaze locked with his. She didn't make any attempt to disguise the conviction of her stance. But deep inside a desperate yearning betrayed her, warning that she secretly hoped to be proven wrong. If Marco noticed the equivocation, he didn't let on. "At least, I hope we'll be happy."

"How can we, *carissima,* when you can't be honest with me?"

"Dammit, Marco!" She shoved back her chair and escaped from behind her desk. He watched her without speaking until her restless pacing came to a stumbling halt in front of her wall chart. For the first time, she saw it through his eyes. It was precise and detailed, each item calculated to the exact day, if not the exact hour. The sheer cold-bloodedness of the thing made her flinch.

"It's quite interesting to have one's entire life displayed on a chart on a wall. I don't think I've ever seen that before." He came up behind her. "Too bad all your secrets aren't recorded so openly."

She turned on him, the anger she'd denied possessing getting the better of her. "You're asking me to trust you with things that I've never told anyone. How am I supposed to do that?"

"I'm your husband."

"A husband I've known for precisely one day." She struggled to remain still beneath the intensity of his scrutiny, but couldn't quite manage it. Spinning around, she ripped the chart from the wall, tossing it in the general direction of her trash basket. She'd retrieve it later, when Marco wasn't around. And this time she'd hide it well away from curious eyes. "There. Satisfied?"

"Not even close. You chose me. You chose to marry me. Does that mean nothing?"

"Of course it means something, but—"

"You can't have it both ways, Hanna. You wanted a husband? Well, now you have one. That means you also have the consequences that come along with it." He seized her shoulders, the passion he'd kept so carefully in check spilling free. "I want a wife, not a companion. I want a future, not a line on someone's chart. I'm not a goal, I'm a man. You can't pencil me in when convenient and erase me when your goals change."

"I wasn't planning on erasing you."

He waved that aside. "Where's your heart, Hanna? Where's your soul? What happened to them?"

"I told you! I don't have a heart. As for my soul, I'm not sure I have one of those, either. I warned you." Her chin wobbled, but she brought it under swift control, praying she hadn't betrayed herself. She wasn't the emotional sort, and it would be disastrous for him to start thinking she was. ''I told you what I expected from our marriage. If you want more than I have to offer, you'll have to find it elsewhere, with someone who can give you love and passion, who can be the sort of woman you need.''

''You're the woman I need.'' He pulled the clasp anchoring her hair free and tossed it aside. Thrusting his hands into the heavy curls, he held the strands to the light so they burned with rich color. ''The passion's there, waiting to be brought out. But you hide it. Are you afraid, is that it?''

She forced herself to remain perfectly still. ''I'm not afraid, because there's nothing to fear. And I told you before, my red hair has nothing to do with whether or not I have a passionate nature. It's a stereotype, the same as redheads having a volatile temper. I married you because it was my goal to find a companionable husband before my twenty-seventh birthday. I've done that.''

His dark eyes contained all the passion she denied possessing. ''So now that we're married, you can cross me off your list?''

"No!" Could he hear the note of pleading in her voice? "Now we can plan for the future. Together."

He released her hair and caught her starched collar instead, urging her a step closer. "Get your pencil, my sweet, so you can record my plans for our future."

"Don't bother. I have excellent recall."

She tried not to inhale his scent, nor to warm herself in his heat or drink in the richness of his dark eyes. But it was so difficult, especially since she wanted to absorb his essence clear down to her bones. He bent so his mouth hovered a fraction above hers.

"I plan to strip you, my lovely swan. I plan to pluck my way through all your feathers until I find the princess hidden underneath. And when I find her, I'm going to make her mine. I don't know what spell holds you captive. But I intend to break it. And when I do, you'll not only discover you have a heart and soul, you'll discover love, too. You won't be in any position to deny it, because it's going to consume you."

For a moment, she almost believed him—believed she was capable of a love that profound, that she could actually experience the sort of emotion he described. He'd planted a seed of longing, one she doubted could be easily weeded from her life. Not that it would grow. Seeds didn't grow on barren soil. Slowly she pulled free. ''Pluck away, Marco. All you'll be left with is feathers. There isn't any princess. There never was.''

''We'll see.''

He didn't let her make good her escape. At the last instant, he captured her with a single kiss, held her as though by enchantment, his lips all that touched her physically. But the sheer force of his personality wrapped her in warmth, bound her tight and nourished her in a way she'd never known nourishment. She was helpless to keep from responding, her mouth parting, opening to him, flowering beneath the intensity of his heat.

He slipped inside, past the barriers to the inner sweetness. She shuddered in reaction, dismayed to discover how easily he overcame her resistance and how quickly and thoroughly he could arouse her. Temptation beckoned, an overwhelming urge to give in to him, to allow the seed he'd planted to flourish, to grow where it had no business taking root.

She murmured in protest, her mind struggling to accomplish what her body couldn't. She fought to deny the pleasure coursing through her, to bring an end to an embrace that would give lie to her stance. She didn't feel anything for this man, at least, nothing more than the companionship she'd claimed. But his mouth stilled the protest, sweeping coherent thought from her head.

Unable to stand the distance between them for another instant, she slid her arms around his neck and pulled him into her. His warmth collided with her, sweeping the chill of loneliness from her body. At long last he put his hands on her, proving beyond any doubt that what she lacked emotionally, she more than made up for through sheer physical desire. Her need for him consumed her, eating through icy exteriors and protective layers like a roaring fire eating through well-seasoned timber. If they'd been anywhere else, she'd have helped him strip away the proper little dress she wore and make quite improper love to her on the top of her desk.

But she was Hanna Tyler and she'd spent her entire life doing what was proper. She'd also spent her life protectively governed by schedules and charts and being as precise as possible. To change now would negate a life's work by those who'd raised her. And she couldn't do that.

"Stop," she whispered. "Please, stop."

He lowered his head, dragging air into his lungs with deep, unsteady breaths. "Tell me we're stopping so we can go someplace more private."

"We're stopping because—" She fought to keep her voice even and dispassionate, to look at him without weeping. "Because I have appointments. I don't have time for...for..." She swept her hand toward the desk, as though he knew she'd actually considered using it for an impromptu bed. "For *this*."

He didn't bother asking for a clearer explanation. Perhaps he'd been considering alternate uses for her desk, too. "So I'm supposed to run along like a good boy until you have an opening in your calendar?"

It wasn't what she'd meant. Not even close. "I have a business to maintain. As soon as I'm finished here, I'll be up to—"

"Don't say it." He stepped well away from her, his eyes burning beneath lowered brows. She'd never known a man who could intimidate with a single look. Until now. "Don't put me in the same category as your business appointments. I told you before I wasn't a gigolo. Trust me, you don't want to start treating me like one. You won't like the results."

Shame filled her. He was right. She'd tried to distance herself using any means possible and he didn't deserve that. "I apologize. I didn't mean to insult you. It's just that I have a schedule to keep. People depend on me." As though to prove her statement, the phone buzzed. "That'll be Pru reminding me that I'm late for my next appointment."

To her relief, he didn't press. "Where should I wait?"

"I have a private apartment upstairs. Make yourself at home."

"Somehow I suspect that'll take more than a single afternoon."

She didn't doubt it for an instant. "As soon as I'm done for the day, I'll be up. We can finish our discussion then."

He continued to study her for an unnerving minute. ''Not only will we finish that discussion, we'll begin quite a few others. You and I have a lot to talk about.''

''No problem.'' Big problem! A full-blown discussion was the one thing she'd do anything to avoid.

Reaching into his pocket, he drew out his hand. It was closed in a fist. Slowly, he unfolded each finger until he'd exposed what he held. A delicate feather rested in the center of his palm. Hanna fought for air. It had to be a feather from the mask she'd worn to the Cinderella Ball or possibly from her costume. How it had ended up in his pocket, she didn't know. But the evidence trembled within his grasp. With infinite grace he lifted his hand to his mouth and blew. The feather exploded into the air between them, carried on the warmth of his breath, whirling and spinning in delicate circles.

''One feather at a time, princess. Until I've stripped them all away,'' he warned. Or was it a threat?

Whichever, she couldn't mistake his meaning. He'd strip away one feather at a time, one secret at a time, until she was naked for the world to see. As far as she was concerned, it was a fate worse than death. It was also a fate she'd resist with every particle of her being.

At least… She'd try.

CHAPTER SIX

IT WAS LATE when Marc awoke, his surroundings pitch-black and unfamiliar. He remained still until he'd regained his bearings and could determine where the hell he was. Then he remembered. He'd fallen asleep in Hanna's living room on her sofa. He sat up with a groan. His head pounded and his stomach grumbled in hunger. He vaguely recalled seeing a lamp on the table beside him and he fumbled in that direction. His memory proved accurate. He flicked the switch, and a harsh glow stabbed through the high-ceilinged room, illuminating the uncomfortable starkness.

Glancing at his watch, he muttered a curse. It was three in the morning and judging by his gut reaction to the utter stillness, Hanna hadn't stepped foot in the place since he'd arrived. The silence felt downright oppressive and he glared in frustration at his surroundings. The room echoed Hanna's claims about herself—at least the self she presented to the world.

157

It was sterile and bland and completely lacking in personality. Although the floor had been laid with a good quality oak, the color had been bleached into nonexistence before being protectively coated with a heavy-duty varnish. A single area rug attempted to add a hint of warmth to the room. It failed miserably, the mottled grays, browns and whites as bland as everything else he'd seen around here. There were a few pictures on the walls, but they were all group photos and not one of them included Hanna. As for the furniture… He winced. It was an eyesore *and* gave him a backache. Two for the price of one. Just great.

Escaping the coldness of the living room, he entered the antiseptic environment of the kitchen. Checking the meager contents of her refrigerator, he decided he could probably throw together a couple of omelettes. If he was hungry, she must be starved by now—starved and too nervous to face him after he'd attacked her with that feather. If it weren't so tragic, it'd be downright amusing.

In addition to the omelette, he peeled an orange for them to share and poured two glasses of wine. Perhaps once he'd fed her, he could coax her to bed, although he was almost afraid to see what her bedroom looked like. No doubt as monastic as the rest of the place. With his luck she'd have a single mattress—too short to fit a decent-sized man—covered with a horse-hair blanket. If so, that would be the first change he instituted.

Ready or not, Hanna was going to find her bed filled with passion.

Loading the food and drinks onto a cutting board that he improvised as a tray, he made his way to her office. Outside her door, he juggled his handful and tapped lightly. Not receiving a response, he walked in.

He found Hanna behind her desk, as he'd expected, and he stood for a long minute, staring. She'd fallen asleep, her glasses askew on her nose, a stack of papers pillowing her cheek, her vivid hair blanketing her arms and shoulders. Even in sleep, tension gripped her, betrayed by the way her hands remained fisted on top of her to-do list. He'd never seen anything so beautiful or so heartbreaking. She was utterly alone amidst a world of precision, a passionate woman stifled by order, the life bled from her until only the brilliance of her hair remained to betray the truth of who and what she was.

He set the tray on the edge of the desk and circled to his wife's side. Ever so carefully, he gathered her up. With a murmur of drowsy contentment, she slipped into his arms as though finding her way home after ages of desperate searching.

"What am I going to do with you?" he asked in tender exasperation.

"Marco?" Her lashes flickered, but didn't quite open. "You came."

"Of course I came. You're my wife."

"Oh." She yawned. "No one's ever come for me before. I usually go to them."

"That's going to change." He glanced at the tray he'd prepared and gave it up. He'd return for it later. Right now, it was time to put his wife to bed. "A lot of things are going to change around here."

"Okay." She yawned. "Take a memo, Pru."

He carried her out of the office. "Pru's not here. I'm the only one left. And since there's no one else currently in charge, I've made a decision." She'd fallen asleep again, not that

it stopped his explanation. "What's the decision, you ask? I'll tell you, *moglie mia*. I've
decided your life is due for a change and it's
up to me to change it. I suppose charts and
graphs and schedules are fine and good."

"Fine and good," she awoke enough to
agree.

"In their place, yes. But you, my sweet,
need a little adventure in your life. Hell, you
need to get a life. And starting tomorrow,
you're going to find that your safe little rut
isn't so safe any more."

"Ruts are fine and good."

He tackled the stairs, his jaw settling into
determined lines. "I promised to pluck the
princess, and by heaven, that's precisely what
I'm going to do. Just so you know, the plucking begins on your twenty-seventh birthday."

She stirred, her hair tickling his chin.
"Happy birthday, Marco."

"Happy birthday to you, wife." He smiled
tenderly at the woman in his arms. "Starting
tomorrow you're going to find what it means
to be married, to be a wife in every sense of
the word, and to have a husband who adores
you."

A wistful expression lent her features a painful vulnerability. "My husband adores me?"

"Yes, my love. I adore you. And I plan to show you how much. There won't be a doubt in anyone's mind that you are the most adored woman in Hidden Harbor. You can deny love for now. But soon, *innamorata,* very soon you'll know that it not only exists. You'll realize it's what you've been waiting for all these years. And it's finally found you."

"Was I lost?"

He carried her through the stark, barren living room. "Yes, Hanna. You were lost. But I've found you now. And I'll never let you go."

"No, don't let go." Her words were slurred with exhaustion.

"Never." He paused by the closed door to her bedroom. "I promise you, love, once I've stripped away the feathers, I'll do whatever it takes to set you free, to help you soar high and far. You'll see. You won't need feathers. It may be trite, but it's true. Love will give you wings." With that, he thrust open the door.

And that's when he found the heart of the princess concealed within the swan.

Her bedroom contained everything the outer trappings of her world denied. Every inch was delightfully feminine and looked like it had been stolen straight from a fairytale. The delicate green carpet spread before him, so thick, it threatened to swallow them whole. The walls were covered in a textured linen paper that reminded him of crisscrossing willow branches. She'd even gotten the furniture right, choosing delicate pieces that were downright pretty. It was a woman's room that reflected a woman's secret dreams and fantasies.

He glanced at the bed, relieved to discover she owned a queen-sized. It would fit two and then some. To his amusement, the delicately carved bedposts supported a transparent gauze canopy that looped and draped, billowing in sensuous waves at the least suggestion of an air current, while a thick goose-down comforter cloaked the mattress in virginal white. He deposited Hanna on the spread, intrigued to see that it cupped her body in silk and lace. Her head dropped onto a silk pillowcase, which suggested her sheets would be silk as well. Marc's smile grew to a grin. He'd been right all along. His innocent bride had

passionate depths hidden beneath her puritan-
ical collar. So much for her claims to the contrary.

As though to emphasize the discrepancy between the properly suited outer woman and the
fiery inner one, Hanna turned toward him, her
hair lapping across the pristine pillow like
waves of flame. ''Marco?''

''Yes?''

''Do you mind if we talk in the morning?
I'd like to go to sleep now.''

''Yes, my sweet. Go to sleep.''

Her lashes lifted and she fixed him with the
direct look he'd long ago realized was her cus-
tom. The color of her eyes had deepened, the
green reminding him of a shrouded glade deep
in a primeval forest, the darkness brightened
with shards of gold, like sunlight darting
through heavy foliage. ''Are you mad at me?''

He perched on the edge of the bed, sinking
into the soft mattress. ''Why in the world
would I be mad at you?''

''Because I've been keeping secrets from
you.''

''It might not have been the best way to begin a marriage.'' He cupped her ankle and

slipped her navy pump from her foot. "But I suspect if we'd had a longer courtship they'd have come out eventually."

"I haven't told you everything."

Her confession came in a nervous little rush and he considered how to respond as he removed her other shoe and set them both on the floor. "You've told me enough. For now."

"Are you going to leave me?"

His brows lifted in astonishment. "Why in the world would I do that?"

"Because I'm not the woman you thought you'd married."

If she only knew. Her eyes had given away more secrets than she realized and no doubt always would. "And what sort of woman is that?" he asked gently.

"I'm not a woman capable of giving you love."

"Why do you think you're incapable of love?"

"I'm not an emotional person, Marco." She stretched with a natural sensuality that belied her words. "I'm logical and precise, not to mention cold and calculating."

He shook his head. She had the oddest opinion of herself. Was she really so blind to her own nature? "We'll deal with that in time." He turned her slightly so he could unzip her dress. Stripping it away—a torturous act that called on every ounce of self-restraint—he swept back the covers and slipped his untouched bride beneath. "Stop worrying and get some sleep."

She rolled onto her side, curling into a ball. Sleep claimed her within seconds, and as it did, her fisted hand relaxed and her fingers unfurled.

And there, dancing delicately in the center of her palm was the feather he'd released in her office.

"Excuse me, but you can't go in there!"

Marc turned to confront the dragon guarding his wife's door. He'd waited until late in the afternoon before making an appearance in the hope that he could coax Hanna from her office without a string of reasons why it would be impossible. By now he expected to find her exhausted and ready for an excuse to end the day. He hadn't realized he'd have to fight his way through more obstacles. First three giants and now a dragon.

He offered his friendliest smile, a smile that had never failed him before, though he suspected today might be a first. "You must be Hanna's secretary."

The woman's eyes narrowed and she scrutinized him with more care than his personal physician. "Damn. I warned her not to marry a charming man. They're nothing but trouble."

He inclined his head, his smile growing wider. "And it will be my great honor to prove it to you."

Her gaze shifted to the gift bag and the huge bouquet of red roses. "What do you have there?"

The one was self-evident, the other none of her business. But he suspected minor details such as that hadn't stopped Pru in the past, nor would they in the future. "Birthday presents for my wife."

"She's the practical sort, you know. She doesn't go in for those feminine gew-gaws. You didn't go and buy her some, did you?"

"Afraid not. But I'll make sure it's at the top of my list for next time." He reached for the doorknob again. "Now if you'll excuse me?"

She fixed him with a stern look. "You hurt her, I'll have something to say about it."

"I expect you will." He fixed her with a look of his own. "And if anyone else hurts her, I'll not only have something to say, I'll have something to *do* about it. Do we have that cleared up?"

She glared at him for a long minute before breaking down and grinning. "I believe we do. Go right in, Mr. Salvatore."

"Marc."

"Call me Pru or Dragonlady. Those are the kindest choices available to you."

"Okay, Pru." He hesitated. "You might want to cancel the rest of Hanna's appointments for the day."

"And why's that?"

"Because she's not going to be here."

"That won't sit well with the Tyler boys. They're due any minute."

"Tough."

Not giving the secretary time to argue, he entered his wife's office. She sat behind her desk, somewhat less comatose than when he'd last found her there. But not by much. She'd traded her severe navy dress for an equally severe gray one. And although her hair wasn't quite as tightly bound as yesterday, he suspected it might have more to do with the headache undoubtedly pounding between her temples than a desire to soften her appearance.

"Hello, Hanna. Happy birthday."

She started, his unexpected appearance clearly catching her by surprise. "Marco. What…?" She slipped off her reading glasses, her attention fastening on the roses. "Are those for me?"

A nasty suspicion dawned on him. "A first?"

"The Tyler boys once gave me a Mother's Day flower arrangement." Her gaze ate up the roses with a deep, bottomless hunger. "But not roses."

"Then let me be the first." He filled her arms with the heady bouquet. The temptation to lean down and capture lips as soft as the rose petals almost got the better of him. He'd have done it, if he didn't suspect it would be a mistake. Hanna didn't deserve to be rushed. Hers would be a leisurely seduction, one she'd

remember her entire life. He dropped the gift
bag on top of her papers. "This is for you,
too."

"You bought me a present plus the roses?"
she asked in a husky voice.

"It's nothing. I didn't have time to find anything too elaborate. Just a small gift for now."

Just a small gift. And yet, it meant the world
to her that he'd be so considerate. She opened
the bag and removed the heart-shaped box she
found inside. He'd had the store wrap it with
a bright red bow and threaded feathers through
the ribbon. She couldn't hide her amusement
as she carefully removed both bow and feathers and opened the box. Inside were the most
delectable chocolates she'd ever seen, each one
a work of art so beautiful, she hesitated to
touch them. "I can't remember when I last had
chocolate."

"So you said. Any special reason?"

"I'm not sure. I think everyone decided it
didn't agree with me."

His eyebrow arced upward. "You break out
in hives? It gives you infections?"

"No," she replied hesitantly, struggling to
recall what she'd been told. "I think it makes

me hyper. But that was years ago, when I was a child. Maybe I could try one and see.''

''Okay. And if something happens, I'll be here to help.''

Hanna didn't doubt that for a minute. ''Thank you.'' She selected a large, thick square of dark chocolate, trimmed with elaborate swirls and colorful flowers. Feeling deliciously guilty, she took a bite. The taste exploded on her tongue and she closed her eyes, sighing in pleasure. This had to be the best thing she'd eaten in a long, long time.

''Good?''

''Oh, Marco. This is wonderful. Have some.''

He leaned against her desk, regarding her with amused indulgence. ''I think it's more fun to watch you.''

''You don't know what you're missing.'' She finished the piece, licking her fingers like a greedy child. Suddenly realizing what she was doing, she snatched a tissue from a nearby box and applied it to her fingertips. ''Sorry. I got carried away.''

He nudged her papers aside and sat fully on the desk, facing her. ''I don't mind. It's nice to see you enjoying yourself.''

"I don't often get the chance to..." She trailed off with a shrug.

"Let your hair down?"

"Something like that."

"Why, Hanna?" he asked. "What's going on around here? You said 'everyone' decided you shouldn't have chocolate. Who is everyone and why would they have any say in what you ate?"

She'd dreaded this moment, when he'd finally begin "plucking." Would he regret marrying her once he knew the truth? Would he leave? Fighting for control, she reached for another chocolate. "Where do you want me to start?"

"How about with the section on your marriage application that listed your parents. Or rather the section that *didn't* list your parents."

She fought for breath. She should have seen this coming and hadn't. Squaring her chin, she forced herself to look at him, offering her calmest, most direct expression. "If you noticed that, there's not much I can add. I don't have any parents. Period. End of discussion."

"Everyone has parents," he pointed out gently. "Even if we're not raised by them. What happened to yours?"

She shrugged, attempting a careless smile and failing miserably. "I don't know."

He didn't say a word. He simply left the desk, scooped her into his arms and sat in her chair, holding her close. She rested her head against his shoulder. She'd never realized how incredible a man's shoulder could feel cushioning her cheek. She glanced up at him, captured within the richness of his brown eyes. For some odd reason, she found herself smiling.

"Did you know that you have irises almost the exact color of the chocolate you bought? Well… Without the flowers and assorted froufrou."

He smiled back at her, the corners of his eyes crinkling. Good grief, but she'd married a gorgeous man. "Think so?"

She nodded. "They look good enough to eat." At the reminder, she twisted around on his lap and reached across her desk for another piece of chocolate, swiping two instead of a more circumspect one. Munching contentedly, she rested her head on his shoulder again. It felt good to sit like this. In fact, it felt really good. "Where was I?"

"You don't know who your parents were and...?"

"And I was raised by various people in town," she retorted briskly. "End of story."

Apparently he couldn't take a hint. "What do you mean various?"

"I mean, everyone took turns."

"*Everyone?* They *all* raised you?"

She sighed. "No, not *all.*" She finished off the chocolate and decided against having another piece, though she really, *really* wanted one. She eyed her messy fingers. Giving in to temptation, she began sucking the chocolate off them. "Only the ones who could provide a proper home got me."

"You mean the authorities didn't choose the most suitable family?" For some reason he sounded outraged.

"See, that was the whole problem." Hanna chuckled. Now that she thought about it, the whole situation was incredibly amusing. Absurd, even. "We're an itty-bitty county. I was the first foster child the town had ever had to deal with. No one could decide who was most suitable to raise me."

"What did they do, draw straws?"

"Nope." She wrinkled her nose at him. "Guess again."

The phone rang before he could. With a groan of exasperation, he snatched it up. "Salvatore."

Hanna frowned. "It's Pru, isn't it? She's calling to warn me that my next appointment is due any minute." Her head throbbed, probably because she'd pulled her hair too tight— as usual. Fumbling for the clasp, she ripped it free, sighing in relief as the curls cascaded over her shoulders. Ah, much better! "Pru'll even tell you the exact time, if you want to hear it. Hour, minute and second. Ask her. You'll see."

"Can't you cancel it?" he questioned instead. Apparently whatever it was couldn't be canceled because he grimaced. Hanna grimaced back. "How long until they get here?" He lifted her arm and checked her watch. "Damn. That doesn't give us very long."

Hanna squinted at her watch, too. For some reason the numbers seemed to be doing a brisk mambo around the dial. "Stop moving!" she ordered. "And tell me what time it is."

Marco frowned again, so she scrunched her face up to match, which only made him frown all the more. She tried to follow suit, but really! A girl could only pucker so far. "Sweetheart? You okay? No, not you, Pru. Hanna's acting strange."

"I am *not* acting strange." She thrust her arm close to his face. "My watch is, see? It's sliding around my wrist. Make it stop doing that."

"Listen, if there's nothing else you can do to stop them, I understand. Ring us when they arrive. I have to take care of Hanna." He slammed the receiver into the cradle. Hooking her chin, he tilted her face upward. "*Carissima?* What's wrong?"

"It's my watch." She shook her arm to show him, surprised at how floppy her wrist and fingers had grown. Marco seemed surprised, too. The clasp held still for a split second and she managed to pry it free. She dangled the watch in front of his nose. "See how big the numbers are? That's so I can see the time at a glance. But now they're bouncing around the dial. Bong, bong, bong. Think you can fix it?"

"It looks fine, Hanna."

"It's broke." She tossed the watch over her head, barely wincing when it smacked against the wall behind her. "Oops. Guess I need a new one."

"You're drunk!" he accused.

"I *am?*" She stretched, laughing out loud. "You know something? I *like* it. I should do this more often."

"Is that why you're not supposed to eat chocolate? Because it makes you drunk?"

Her mouth dropped open. "Really? No one told me that." Another laugh bubbled up and she covered her lips to contain it. Not that it did any good. It escaped through her fingers in a breathless rush. "I want more."

"Not a chance, *cara*. You've had quite enough."

"If you give me another piece, I'll tell you about Henry Tyler," she wheedled.

"Tell me about Henry Tyler, anyway."

"Okay, but you can't let on I squealed." She lifted a finger to her lips. At least, she hoped they were her lips. They felt oddly numb. "Shhhh. Promise?"

"Cross my heart."

"Not even the boys know."

"I'm honored you'd confide in me."

She peeked around to make sure no one else was listening. A person could never be too careful. For instance, the philodendron decorating her desk looked entirely too interested in their conversation, so she lowered her voice. "I married Henry so the boys wouldn't lose the farm," she confided.

"I don't understand."

She stared at him, thoroughly disappointed. "I thought you were smart."

"I'm very smart, my sweet. But you're a wee bit drunk." He shrugged. "Sometimes that makes communication a tad difficult."

"Oh. Okay." She captured one of his shirt buttons and gave it a twist. "You see, Henry got sick and didn't have insurance to pay for his medical bills. If I hadn't married him, the boys would have had to sell the farm to pay off his debts."

"And instead he married you?"

"He didn't want to." Her mouth pulled down at the corners and she twisted his button some more. It came off in her hand and she peeped up at him to see if he'd noticed.

Unfortunately, he had. "Oops," she said with a weak grin.

"Never mind that. Just explain about Henry."

She tossed the button over her head, grinning when it pinged off the wall and joined her watch on the floor. "He still loved his deceased wife, Marcy. But I told him it was the only way to protect the boys' inheritance." She tackled the next button. "And I did owe him, though I didn't tell him that. Probably would have sunk the whole deal if I had."

"You owed him?"

"Oh, dear. Wasn't supposed to tell you that, either." She let go of his button and pretended to zip her lips together. For some reason, they wouldn't stay that way. The words kept tumbling out with far too much honesty and far too little control. "Maybe if he hadn't been so sick, he'd have argued better. But I'm real logical. So he gave in."

"Let me get this straight. You married Henry Tyler so you could pay his bills?"

She gave his button a sharp tug. "Be quiet! Someone might hear." She looked around again, shooting the listening plant a warning glare. Satisfied, she whispered, "The boys wouldn't take the money if they knew the truth. They have pride, you know. They'd sell the farm in order to pay me back." The second button snapped off in her hand and she tossed that aside, too. "Don't you get it? I'm real good at making money. They needed some. I had lots of extra sitting around doing nothing. Seems fair, right?"

"That was a sweet, generous thing to do."

She grinned. "I'm full of secrets. Aren't I?"

"Without question. Do you have any more you want to tell me about?"

"Maybe." She gave him a calculating look. "Wanna feed me more chocolate so you can find out?"

"Do I have to?" He stopped her from attacking his next button, ignoring her pouting reprimand. "Why don't you just tell me."

She sighed. "You're really good at this," she complained. "Okay. I have lots of secrets."

"Like what?"

"Like…" She glanced at him from beneath her lashes. "Like I like sitting on your lap. I've never sat on a man's lap before."

"I'm afraid I'll have to limit you to one man's lap from now on," he warned.

"Oh, I don't mind. It's a good lap." She blew out her breath, thrusting her hair from her face. How the heck had it gotten there, anyway? She was always so careful to keep it tied back. "What else? You're really cute, you know. Though I guess that's no secret."

"Still... It's nice that you think so," he offered judiciously.

"Want to guess what else?"

He shook his head. "Tell me."

Her gaze fastened on his mouth. It was such a delicious mouth, full, broad and very, very clever. "I get all gushy inside when you kiss me. Bet I kept that a secret."

"Right up until now," he said with a grin. Truth be told, it was a sexy little grin that perfectly matched his delicious mouth, a grin that tempted her to cover it with her lips and claim it for her own. "If it makes you feel any better, I get...er...gushy, too."

"Does it make you want to take off your clothes?" she asked curiously.

"Actually, it makes me want to take off *your* clothes."

"Oh. I suppose you could go ahead and do that." She began fumbling with the buttons of her dress. "Maybe I can help."

"Here? In your office?" Just as she started making progress his hands covered hers, making it tough to work through the confusing length of buttons and holes. "Your stepsons are due any minute now."

"That's okay. They can wait until we're done."

"Tell me something, Hanna. Have you ever made love before?"

She began to giggle and slapped a hand over her mouth again. "You caught me," she said, her voice muffled.

Gently, he pried her fingers free, his gaze unbelievably tender. "What did I catch you at?"

"I've never made love in my office before."

"Or anywhere else?"

"Nope. Not there, either."

"Well, a desk might not be the best place to start."

She gave that serious consideration. "I know where there's a sofa."

The phone on her desk rang and she snatched up. "Hello?" she trilled gaily. Frowning, she shook the receiver. "Oh, pooh. It's not working."

"Try it this way, *carissima.*" He turned the receiver around.

"Hello?" she trilled again.

"Mrs. Tyler?"

"Used to be. How's it hangin', Pru?"

"Quite well, thank you. I just called to tell you it's three o'clock and your sons have arrived."

"It's three?"

There was a momentary silence. "Actually, it's two fifty-eight. Remember? I called a few minutes ago to—"

"Whatever," Hanna interrupted breezily. "Don't think I've ever lost track of time before. Well, except when I got married."

"You... You lost track of time? *Again?*"

There was a whispered conversation and she heard the boys starting to shout. Wincing, Hanna held the phone away from her ear. "What do you mean she lost track?" came clearly through the receiver.

Pru cleared her throat. "Also, I wanted to remind you that Mother and Father Henderson are expecting you to join them at six for dinner."

"Got lots of mothers and fathers. Which ones are they?"

"I...I told you. The Hender—"

"Too bad. Cancel my appointments."

"I beg your pardon?"

"I always wanted to say that," she confided to Marco, before returning her attention to the phone. "Cancel 'em. And cancel tomorrow's, too."

There was another whispered conversation, followed by a roar that could be heard right through her solid oak door.

"Uh-oh," she said. Carefully, she hung the phone up. "Maybe they'll think it was a bad connection."

Marco reached past her, removed the receiver from the philodendron and returned it to the cradle. "I'm afraid they won't." He sighed. "I think that roar was our signal to go, sweet. Where shall we take the party?"

"You go out there—" she waved in the general direction of the door "—and take the steps up.'' Her brow puckered. ''Can't quite remember where those darned stairs got to, but I'm pretty sure they're around here some-place.''

''Hang on.'' Before she had a chance to re-act, he stood, swinging her high against his chest. ''Put your arms around my shoulders and hold on tight.''

''Okay.'' She flung her arms around his neck with more enthusiasm than grace. He choked a bit and she eased her grip. Wouldn't do to strangle her brand-new husband. She kind of liked having him around. ''What now?''

''No matter what happens, don't let go. Got it?''

''Got it.'' She tried to wink, but her eyes didn't seem to be working too well. First one shut, then the other. Finally, she gave up and left them that way. With a contented sigh, she dropped her head to his shoulder again. Perfect. Life was absolutely perfect.

Marco crossed the room with impressive speed, threw open the door and plunged into the crowd blocking her doorway.

''What the hell's going on?'' Jeb shouted.

"What have you done to Hanna?"

"She forgot the time!"

"And look at her hair. He's...he's... Dammit all! He's been in there seducing her."

Hanna pried her eyes open. "Steps," she announced, pointing. "I found them. Go thatta way. Hey! I just remembered. There's a bed up there. And a sofa, too. We'll have lots of choices."

Josie disappeared into her office, reappearing a moment later with the box of candy in his hands. "Look what he gave her."

"You fed her chocolate?" Jeb reeled around. "You *bastard!*"

"Pru, cancel the rest of Hanna's appointments," Marco ordered the secretary. "And clear the building. Brew a pot of coffee, if you would. Hot, strong and black. Bring it up as soon as it's ready."

"You can't tell everyone what to do!" Janus protested.

"Watch me," Marco snapped. "You have your instructions, Pru."

"Yes, sir," the woman replied. "I gather Mrs. Tyler isn't feeling well?"

"She's feeling great. Too great." Marco hesitated at the foot of the steps leading to Hanna's quarters. Swinging around he scrutinized the occupants of the reception area with a dangerous gleam in his eyes. "And it's Salvatore. Hanna Salvatore. You don't want to forget again."

"That's right," Hanna piped up. "Or he'll do that Italian thing on you." She tightened her arms around him. "Come on. Let's go upstairs so you can do that Italian thing on me."

CHAPTER SEVEN

THE DOOR TO HANNA'S apartment wasn't locked, which came as a relief to Marc, considering he had about five seconds before all hell broke loose. It took a moment to juggle his armful, open the door and get them both inside. But he managed, and before the oddball collection of "sons" gathered their wits sufficiently to interfere.

Stepping over the threshold, he slammed the door closed and threw the lock in the hope of ensuring their privacy, though he suspected the Dragonlady would prove a more successful barrier than the dead bolt. Once again, he carried his bride to the bedroom—a bride he had absolutely no intention of touching. It was enough to drive a newlywed husband insane. Ever so gently he deposited his precious—not to mention tipsy—armful in the center of her snow-white bed. She'd hung her swan princess mask from the post, he noticed with wry amusement. Was it a warning that she wouldn't be easily plucked? Or could it be an invitation?

"Are you going to make love to me?" she asked curiously.

"Not tonight."

"Oh." She reached out and touched the mask, her breath catching when two white feathers came loose and drifted onto the mattress beside her. "Is it because I ate chocolate?"

He selected the larger of the two feathers and brushed it across her lips. "Something like that."

"Oh," she said again, shivering beneath the silky caress. She actually looked disappointed and he took it as an encouraging sign. "Perhaps if things had been different...?"

He didn't pretend to misunderstand. "No perhaps about it." He slid the feather from her mouth to her cheek and her eyes fluttered closed. Sleep wouldn't be far behind.

"But not tonight," she whispered.

"I'd be taking advantage of you."

"And that's wrong, right?"

"Very wrong." He gritted his teeth, his self-control stretched painfully thin. Time to end this before it shredded beyond repair. "I know it's early, but sleep is the best thing for you. I'll tell Pru to cancel the coffee."

She yawned. "I am tired."

"You'd be more comfortable if you took off your dress, Hanna."

"Okay."

She made no move to take care of it and he swore beneath his breath. *"Bella mia?"*

"I'm too tired. Maybe if I had some more chocolate?" Her lashes lifted and she peeked up at him with a greedy expression. "Did you bring any up?"

"I'm afraid Jeb-Janus-Josie confiscated it."

"No chocolate. Shoot." Her brow puckered in a frown for a brief instant, before clearing. "Jeb-Janus-Josie? You're not having trouble telling my sons apart, are you?"

"Stepsons."

Setting the feather carefully on her nightstand, he crossed to her dresser and tugged open drawers at random. The interiors were as neat and tidy as everything else about his darling wife. They were also revealing. Just like the difference between her spartan apartment and sumptuous bedroom, her austere dresses concealed the most sensuous bits of silk and lace. He selected a nightgown, a long transparent slip of ivory that drifted through his fingers like wisps of fog.

"And yes, I'm having trouble telling them apart." He approached, her nightgown floating in his hand. "Although, I've figured out the one with the big muscles and even bigger attitude is Jeb."

"He's not so bad once you get to know him."

"I'll keep that in mind." He offered the nightgown. "Need help?"

She sat up with a grimace. "I can handle it."

His mouth tilted upward. "Probably for the best." Definitely for the best. She glanced at him again, words trembling on her lips. "What is it, sweetheart?" he prompted.

"Do you remember the room where we were married?"

"Sure."

"It was pretty, wasn't it?"

"Very pretty. Homey, I'd say."

"It *was* like a home," she agreed, tucking her legs beneath her. "It would be nice to have a place like that, don't you think?"

Actually, it reminded him a bit of her bedroom. Didn't she see that? "If that's what you prefer, why live here?"

"Because it's practical."

"Practical." He sighed. Naturally. He handed over the nightgown. "Sleep well, Hanna."

She clutched the scrap of silk to her chest and all he could picture was rose-tipped ivory skin encased in that breath of nothing. Stifling a groan, he forced himself to cross the endless expanse of pale green carpeting. She stopped him before he could make good his escape. "Marco?"

He paused at her bedroom door. If he didn't leave soon, he'd end up giving in to the less-than-honorable part of his nature. Hanna didn't deserve that. Not after what he'd learned today. He leaned his forehead against the door, one hand gripping the knob so hard it was a wonder it didn't crack off in his hand. "Yes, love?"

"It's hard being practical all the time."

"I can imagine. I'll see if I can't help you overcome that particular character flaw."

"Thank you," she whispered. "But I'm afraid you might be too late."

He opened the door. "Trust me, Hanna. I'm not too late. And it'll be my pleasure to prove it to you. Just not tonight." Quietly, he shut the door behind him. No, not tonight. But, soon. He'd prove it to her very soon. With a bit of luck, he'd even manage it before he went totally insane.

Or maybe with a whole lot of luck.

To Marc's surprise, the "Dragonlady" helped with his next adventure.

"Kidnap her," Pru repeated. "You want to kidnap your own wife? What the hell for?"

"She needs a little excitement in her life. She also needs to get away from her responsibilities for a day and discover there's more to life than work. Now are you going to help me, or do I have to do this in spite of you?"

"Oh, I'll help." She pursed her lips. "In fact, you might even turn out to be good for her, despite your shortcomings."

He didn't bother asking what those shortcomings were. Knowing Pru, she'd be only too happy to catalogue them. "I don't want anyone else interfering, which is where you come in.''

''Need me to run interference for you, huh? No surprise there.''

Marc stifled the urge to wring the old woman's neck. ''Can you keep the Tyler boys away from the office until after I've kidnapped Hanna?''

''They *have* been hanging around more than usual.'' Pru's smile took on a malicious tilt. ''For some reason they don't trust you. Why do you suppose that is, charm boy?''

''Obviously you've misjudged me,'' he returned smoothly. ''I guess I'm not as charming as you'd like to believe.''

She actually broke down and grinned. ''Oh, well. Nobody's perfect. Okay. I'll make some calls and keep the boys tied up for the next hour or so. Think you can get yourself organized by then or do you need help with that, too?''

''It'll be tough,'' he said in a dry voice. ''But I'll manage.''

Pru checked her watch. ''One hour, Salvatore. The clock's ticking. After that, you're on your own.''

No doubt she'd hold him to the minute, too. What was it with people and time around here? "An hour's all I need." He hoped.

Fortunately, he'd put the majority of the plan into motion before approaching Pru. He just had to finalize the details and pack. As it turned out, once he'd finished even those few chores, he had precisely ten minutes to spare. When he returned downstairs, Pru made a production of checking her watch. Satisfied, she gave him the once-over.

"Glad to see you know enough to wear black to a kidnapping." She tossed the black scarf he'd used at the Cinderella Ball in his direction. "But if you're going to snatch her, you ought to do it right."

"Where the hell did you get this?" he demanded.

"You think I have this job because of my pretty face?"

He knew better than to respond to that. Without a word, he tied the scarf around his head and adjusted the eyeholes so he wouldn't crash into a wall. No doubt he looked like a total idiot. It was one thing to wear the scarf at the Cinderella Ball. But here, in broad daylight... Somehow he suspected it lost a lot in the translation. "Satisfied?" he asked.

Pru's amusement died and a wistful expression gleamed in her eyes. "Yeah, you'll do. One more thing..." This time she offered a lightweight rope. "Like I said. If you're gonna kidnap her—"

Marc fought for restraint. "I ought to do it right?"

"You got it."

"You're trying to get me arrested, aren't you?"

"As tempting as that notion is, I'm not. In fact, I called the local sheriff's office to warn them what you were up to. They'll probably stop laughing next week."

"Oh, great. Did you call the local paper, too?"

"Sure did. You can put the photos in your wedding album. It'll be a tale to tell the kiddies."

"Thanks," he said through clenched teeth. Though he did take heart in the fact that she anticipated kids in his future with Hanna.

"You'd better thank me, Salvatore. You wouldn't have gotten two blocks without my help. Everyone in Hidden Harbor knows Hanna. They wouldn't take kindly to a mysterious stranger up and stealing her away.''

''Even if it's her husband?''

''Especially if it's her husband. You already have everyone in a tizzy, wondering whether you're going to take her away with you to whichever foreign city you hail from.''

''San Francisco isn't a foreign city.''

She snorted. ''It is when you live on the east coast. Hell, Baltimore is a foreign city to us. We want to keep Hanna right here. We found her. We're keeping her.''

''What do you mean you fou—''

Pru tapped her watch. ''Time's up, charm boy. You have precisely sixty seconds to pack up your bride and get her out of here before the Tylers arrive. That's if you're lucky.'' She gave him another of her malicious smiles. ''But, I'm bettin' your luck's just run out.''

Swearing under his breath, he thrust open Hanna's door. She was wearing those atrocious reading glasses and she looked up in astonishment when he bolted into the room. ''Marco? Is that you?''

"Sorry, *cara*. We need to move this along. Could you stand, please?"

"What's going on? I don't have time—"

"Yes, yes, I know. You never have time. Unfortunately, I don't have time, either. So since neither of us has any...." He caught her hand and yanked her from the chair. Whipping her glasses from the tip of her nose, he tossed them aside. Next he swiftly looped the rope around first one wrist, then the other, tying them with a couple of careless knots. Finished, he tossed her over his shoulder. "I'm in a bit of a hurry, I'm afraid."

"*Marco!* Put me down. You can't do this. I have work. I have clients."

"So I've noticed. You also have charts and schedules and plans." He carried her into the reception area. "Lots and lots of plans."

"Pru!" She shoved her hands against his back. "Do something."

"I already have, Hanna. I told your stepsons you were being kidnapped. They should be along..." She checked her watch once more. "Oh...right about now."

Marc let loose with a swear word that no doubt turned his genteel Southern bride's ears pink. Moving as quickly as safety allowed, he headed down the steps and out of the building. He hit the sidewalk the same instant as the Tylers pulled up in a battered pickup. The expression on their faces was an identical look of shock and fury. They also shouted the exact same curse, one Marc resented for his mother's sake. Whoever said people in the south took life at a more leisurely pace hadn't visited Hidden Harbor.

With a mere fifteen seconds left to his allotted hour, Marc tossed Hanna into the backseat of the convertible he'd rented. Ignoring her shrieks of outrage, he vaulted behind the steering wheel in true Zorro fashion. If he hadn't left the key in the ignition, he doubted he'd have escaped in time. As it was, he almost knocked over Jeb as he roared away from the curb. Of course, if he'd actually hit the man, the convertible would have been totaled. Jeb, no doubt would have walked away without a scratch.

His sweet bride managed to fight her way into an upright position. ''Have you lost your ever-loving mind? What are you doing?''

"I thought that was obvious." He risked a quick glance over his shoulder and fought to suppress a grin. Apparently, her hair hadn't taken kindly to being turned upside down and dumped in the rear of a fast-moving car, particularly one without a top. While Hanna busily gnawed at the ropes restraining her wrists, her hair exploded around her like an erupting volcano. "I'm kidnapping you."

"Would you mind telling me *why* you're kidnapping me?"

"Not at all. I decided we deserved a honeymoon. And since I knew you wouldn't agree, at least not without three or four years advance notification, I took it upon myself to rearrange your schedule."

"A honeymoon?" He couldn't quite tell whether the idea thrilled her or elicited something akin to horror.

"That's right. A honeymoon. You know.... One of those occasions that usually comes immediately after the wedding and shortly before the babies. At least, it does if you get it in the appropriate order."

"Babies?"

"Sorry, my sweet. I didn't mean to scare you."

"So we won't be going directly from our honeymoon to an obstetrician?"

She'd recovered her sense of humor, he was relieved to note. "Not unless we get real lucky."

"Lucky." Hanna leaned over the seat, strands of her hair wrapping around him. If her wrists weren't tied, it probably would have been her hands around his neck instead of her hair. "How did we go from the Cinderella Ball to babies? What happened to our trial marriage? In case you've forgotten, you're still my bridegroom-on-approval. And I'm not sure I approve."

He'd hoped she'd given up on that idea. He should have known better. His wife hadn't quite gotten the hang of "happily-ever-after" yet. Nor had she relaxed her guard enough to enjoy wedded bliss. Perhaps after tonight that would change. Something had to. He was getting tired of carting her from office to bed at three each morning and finding her long gone when he awoke the next day. She couldn't keep up the pace without damaging her health and he couldn't spend another night in their bed without making love to her.

"You asked for a trial marriage and I agreed," Marc conceded. "But so far all we've had is the trial without any of the marriage."

"I assume by this little kidnapping scheme that you're planning to change that?"

"If you don't mind."

"And if I do?"

He pulled the car to the side of the road and killed the engine. Holding out his hand, he helped Hanna climb into the bucket seat beside him. He first freed her hands and then removed his mask. "Here. You can use the scarf to tie your hair."

"Again."

"Yes, again." He studied her for a long moment. Faint lilac smudges underlined her eyes emphasizing the paleness of her skin. He knew the early signs of exhaustion when he saw it. "This has to end, Hanna. Either we make an effort to create a real marriage or we call it quits, no harm done. You go back to your clocks and timetables and appointment books. Choose one of the steroid-enhanced peacocks constantly being paraded through your office. And continue on with your sterile life.''

She fixed her gaze on the front windshield. If it hadn't been for the faint tremor of her chin, he'd have sworn his words hadn't made any impression. ''Or?'' she finally asked.

''Or you can go away with me for the next two days.'' He tied her hair back with his scarf, knotting it at the nape of her neck. A wayward curl danced at her temple and unable to resist, he smoothed it from her face. ''What do you say, Hanna? We can get to know each other. I can feed you more chocolate and you can spill your secrets.''

A smile flirted with her mouth. ''I'd rather avoid the chocolate, if you don't mind. Once was quite enough.''

''Agreed. In that case, you can spill your secrets without the chocolate.''

''All of them?'' she whispered, bowing her head.

''Well... Maybe just one or two more.''

She turned and looked at him, her eyes full of spring greens and autumnal golds, the colors echoing the depth and richness of both seasons. "You'll want to make love to me, won't you?"

"Yes."

"I've wanted to make love to you from the first time I saw you," she admitted with devastating frankness.

"The feeling's mutual."

"Marco?"

"Yes, my sweet?"

"If you don't want my stepsons killing you, I think you'd better get us out of here."

Marc glanced over his shoulder and swore. The Tyler boys had finally caught up with them, their rattletrap bearing down with all the determination its rusty innards could muster. "Fasten your seat belt, Hanna. Time to go." He started the engine and floored it, leaving Jeb-Janus-and-Josie choking on an impressive plume of dust. Hanna swivelled in her seat and gave them a reassuring thumbs up. Marc restrained from also giving them a finger, especially since it would be a slightly different version than his wife's. He checked the mirror again, his mouth tightening. When he returned from his honeymoon, he'd deal with that situation once and for all.

"So where are we going?" Hanna asked.

"I rented a cottage a little north of here. I checked it out yesterday to make sure it would do." He grinned. "See? You're not the only one who can plan."

"I'm impressed."

The cottage offered the best of two worlds—sea and woods. Tucked snugly into the edge of a pine forest, the decks off the front of the house provided a sweeping view of the ocean. The cottage was small, but charming. The first floor had an open-style kitchen and a huge living room, one wall of which was an enormous stone fireplace. Marc left Hanna to explore while he unloaded their suitcase from the trunk of the car and carried it upstairs to the only bedroom the cottage boasted.

He'd given particular attention to the appearance of this room, more so than any other part of the house, wanting it to echo what Hanna had created at home. No doubt the real estate agent who'd shown him the various rental cottages had thought him insane, since the first place he'd checked had been the bedroom. But he didn't give a damn. It had taken most of the day and nearly a dozen stops before he'd found this place. The second he'd set eyes on the four-poster canopied bed and white lace coverings, he'd known Hanna could relax here.

She appeared in the doorway to the bedroom and took a long minute to prowl around, poking through the closets and dresser before stepping out onto the small balcony. She finished off her exploration by dropping onto the mattress. "Oh, my," she said, turning a satisfied smile in his direction. "This is absolutely perfect."

"I thought you'd like it."

"And you packed for both of us?"

"Hope you don't mind." He set the suitcase onto a mahogany stand and unzipped it. "A cold front's moving down from the north tonight, so I wanted to make sure you had something warm to wear tomorrow."

She perked up. "Does that mean we can have a fire?"

"Sure thing."

"The office building doesn't have a fireplace. I wish it did."

"Maybe we can have one installed." He leaned against the bedposts, pleased to notice the lines of tension easing from her face. "Or maybe we can get a real house instead of living in a converted factory."

For a moment, her expression turned wistful and he remembered their conversation the night he'd fed her the chocolate—how she'd wished for a house like the room in which they'd been married. "When I was a little girl, I used to dream of having my own place."

"What else did you dream about?" he asked gently.

At first, he didn't think she'd answer. When she did, he had to strain to hear her words. "I dreamt of a big, old-fashioned home." Her glance was as direct as ever, amusement emphasizing the soft green color. "You know the type I mean? With the decorative wooden trim painted in pastels. And a big old porch with a wooden swing for two."

"And who'd be sitting on that swing with you?"

"My husband. And maybe a baby or two." Her laughter held a hint of self-derision. "Silly, isn't it? In this day and age I should be dreaming about a high-powered career and a staff of employees instead of something straight out of the fifties.''

''You have a high-powered career and a staff of employees. We're talking about dreams, not reality.''

She straightened, her expression settling into remote lines. ''Actually we were talking about childhood dreams. The kind that never come true. The kind you don't need anymore once you're an adult.''

''So you don't want a house?''

She shrugged. ''Why, when I have the office?''

''Ever practical. Right, Hanna?''

''Absolutely.''

''And the husband? No, wait.'' He snapped his fingers. ''I almost forgot. I'm the husband.''

''Sarcasm, Marco?''

He didn't bother answering, since he figured his tone was self-evident. ''What about the children, Hanna? Have you thought about them?''

''I've thought about the possibility. But right now I barely have time for you. I don't think we'd be wise to add a baby to the mix.

Babies take a lot of care. They need time and attention. You can't just want them one minute and toss them aside the next when they become too much trouble. You can't just—'' Her voice broke and she stared at him with stricken eyes.

He straightened. ''Hanna?''

''I—'' Her voice failed her again and he started toward her, but she tumbled from the bed, warding him off with upheld hands. ''I'm sorry, Marc. I don't know what's gotten into me. I guess the late nights are finally catching up.''

She'd called him Marc instead of Marco. That, more than anything else, kept him from touching her. He wanted to push, to demand that she explain what was wrong. But he didn't dare. *You're the patient Salvatore,* he reminded himself. And pushing Hanna wouldn't elicit as positive a response as coaxing. Reining in his need to take charge and force answers to his questions, he simply said, ''In that case, we'll have to make sure you have plenty of opportunity to relax.''

''Thank you,'' she whispered gruffly.

His mouth pulled to one side. "For what? Giving you a chance to relax or letting you off the hook?"

Reluctant laughter gleamed in her eyes. "Yes."

"Got it. Hungry? Would you like some lunch?"

"How about a phone? I have to check in with Pru—"

"Not a chance."

"But—"

He cut her off with a single look. "What will happen if you take a day off?"

"Marco, you can't simply swoop down and carry me off when the mood takes you," she complained.

"Why not?"

"Because I have responsibilities. People are depending on me. You might not have any business concerns to worry about, but I do."

He went rigid, annoyance beginning a slow simmer. "What makes you say I don't have any business concerns?"

She shrugged. "I know you told me you were some sort of salesman. I guess that gives you more free time than it gives me." She gestured to indicate the room. "This was a sweet idea, but I can't leave everything at the office without making advance arrangements."

"You just did. The world won't end because you walked away from work. Nor is work the same as having a life."

"I have people depending on me."

"So do I."

That stopped her. "Really? You never said anything."

"You never asked."

A hint of color mounted her cheeks. "You're right. I haven't. I apologize."

"I don't want an apology. In case you haven't noticed, I want a wife. Do you want to be my wife, Hanna?"

He saw it again, that wistful longing for some unobtainable dream. Was he like the gingerbread house with the white picket fence and porch swing she'd described? Is that why she'd set herself a goal to marry in five years, because a husband symbolized all she longed to possess? Well, he wasn't a symbol, any more than he was a line on a graph. He was a man and her husband. And tonight she'd have that fact brought home.

"You haven't answered my question," he prompted. "Who are you going to put first today, your business or your husband? Just one day, Hanna. That's all I'm asking."

Her hands closed into fists and he knew she fought a fierce inner battle. He didn't doubt for a minute that her entire life she'd put business ahead of pleasure, denying what she most needed. But the desire was there, burning so brightly it was a wonder it didn't set her aflame.

"You come first."

At least she didn't add, "today." His mood right now was uncertain at best and that one, simple word would have been just enough to push him over the edge. This was supposed to be a romantic two days. Marc doubted Hanna would find anything romantic about his losing the infamous Salvatore temper.

"Thank you," he said. Unable to resist, he gathered her close and kissed her.

There was so much sweetness in her, so much warmth and passion. If only he could find a way to push past the barriers she was constantly erecting. As though reading his thoughts, she pulled back and murmured something about unpacking. He let her go. He could afford to be patient a little longer.

Maybe.

CHAPTER EIGHT

THEY SHOULD HAVE brought chocolate.

"Would you care for anything else to eat?" Hanna asked politely. She desperately wanted to break through the barriers between them—defensive barriers she'd slammed into place the minute he'd kissed her and couldn't seem to lower no matter how hard she tried.

"No, thank you," Marco answered, every bit as politely.

"A drink?"

"There's a bottle of champagne in the refrigerator. Would you care for a glass?"

The offer was tempting. Too tempting. "Perhaps later, thanks."

"Hanna—"

He'd finally lost patience with her. And why not? She'd lost patience with herself. "This is ridiculous!" She threw down her napkin and shot out of her chair. Wrapping her arms around her waist, she stalked into the living room, pacing in front of the barren hearth.

"Why are we even bothering, Marco? We have nothing in common. You're West coast, I'm East. You're a family man, I'm a career woman. I'm meticulous and driven, which drives you crazy."

He came after her, moving with an easy, masculine grace that had attracted her from the beginning. He was everything she'd always wanted in a man, starting on the outside and working in to the very core of him. Tall, lean, devastatingly handsome, she couldn't look at him without suffering from an overwhelming urge to touch him. He was also patient and sincere and honest. Not to mention kind. So incredibly kind. But there was something more. Something that touched her on a deeper level. His every word echoed with a depth of passion that precisely matched what raged in her own heart. How was that possible? How could two such opposite people be so perfectly mated?

"Stop thinking, Hanna."

Humor momentarily overrode her concern. "It's what I do best."

"It's what you've been trained to do." He stopped scant inches away, not touching her, yet wrapping her in the warmth of his presence. "I know you have a mind. I know you're a smart, dedicated woman. But I also know you have a heart and soul."

A pained laugh broke from her. "Then you know more than I do."

"Why do you say that?" He leaned into her, drugging her with his essence. "What makes you think you aren't capable of love?"

She stepped back, determined not to be influenced by whatever spell he wove every time he came near. "I don't trust love! It's not real. You can have it safely in hand one day and the next morning the sun comes up and you discover love's vanished with the night."

"Is that what happened?" His compassion threatened to undo her. "Did love vanish on you?"

"Yes," she whispered.

"And you're afraid that I'm going to disappear, too?"

"I don't want to wake up one morning and find you've left. I—" She fought for control. Where the *hell* had it gone? She'd always been able to summon it with such ease. But ever since meeting Marco, it had deserted her with alarming regularity. "I don't think I could handle it."

Still he didn't touch her, just holding her with the warmth of his gaze. "There's nothing I can say to ease your fears, *innamorata*. You know that, don't you?"

She nodded. Unfortunately, she did.

"I can make all the promises in the world and they won't be worth anything without trust." He leaned his shoulder against the fireplace mantle and folded his arms across his chest. So he wouldn't be tempted to wrap them around her? she couldn't help but wonder. She could read between the lines. He was going to make her deal with this on her own, without exerting undue influence. "We haven't known each other long, which makes it even more difficult. But I'm telling you that what we feel toward each other is rare. More rare than you can imagine."

"I suspected as much," she confessed.

"The problem is... Our relationship is forcing you to operate on instinct and you're not accustomed to that."

"Not even a little."

"But trust comes from those instincts. Either you believe in me or you don't. Either you trust what I tell you or you don't. Either you listen to what your heart tells you or you allow logic and practicality to dictate your life."

"I want to believe you," she whispered. More than anything, she wanted to trust Marco.

"You can't just want, you have to do it." He did touch her then, gathering her face within his palms, his gaze so understanding it tore her apart. "There will come a day when you'll be forced to make a choice between your head and your heart. Your head will tell you to doubt. To run. And that's when you'll face an irrevocable decision. You'll have to trust. When everyone and everything around you is screaming for you to doubt, you'll have to take that leap of faith. Make the wrong choice and you'll regret it for the rest of your life."

She knew what he referred to. Already, a little voice was screaming for her to trust him, begging her not to ruin this chance for a happy future because the past had instilled fears she battled to this day. At the same time, the rational, sensible part of her flashed danger signals so loud, they drowned out that little voice. ''And you expect me to go with my gut feelings rather than with common sense?''

He smiled, a beautifully tender smile. ''If you love someone, you trust them. It's that simple and that difficult. If your love is true, you know the person you gift with that love will never do anything to deliberately hurt you. True love doesn't disappear in the night, Hanna. It flourishes beneath the warmth of the sun and holds strong through the darkness of night.''

''Haven't you ever had doubts?''

He inclined his head. ''Of course. Life is strewn with pebbles and rocks and boulders. You know that as well as I. But I'd like to think that love can help you find a path over or around or through those adversities. When one person slips, the other is there to lend a hand. Haven't you found, even during the most difficult days, that people are there for you? People who love you?''

''Yes.'' No question. The residents of Hidden Harbor had done that for her and more.

"And aren't you there for them in their time of need?"

"I try to be."

"Don't you see? We can have that, too, Hanna. Let me in. I won't hurt you, I swear it."

He didn't understand. "What if *I* hurt *you?*"

"I'll deal with that if it happens."

Her mouth twisted. "Don't you mean when?"

"I sincerely hope not." He stepped back, his arms falling to his sides. "Come to me, Hanna. But come of your own free will. Come because you want me, because you choose to be my wife."

For a split second, apprehension held her in place. She had precisely two options: Marco or the life she'd led up until now. The utter simplicity of her decision hit her. She was wrong. There weren't two options. There never had been. This man was the one she'd been awaiting all these years, the one she'd longed to find.

She flew into his arms, surrendering to a need far greater than fear, to a passion that defied logic and sensibility, that couldn't be charted or graphed or neatly entered into her schedule. Her feelings for Marco were sprawling and messy and fell outside all boundaries. Time had no meaning. Planning was utterly useless. It left her with one option. She went with her instincts, trusting where she'd never dared trust before.

His arms enfolded her, holding her so close their heartbeats melded. The next instant, it was their lips melding, his life-giving breath becoming hers. ''You could have had anyone,'' she whispered brokenly.

''You were the one I wanted. The only one I've ever wanted.''

''*Why?*''

''Whether or not you know it, you're my soul mate, the one woman who completes me. Run, hide, deny what's between us,'' he said fiercely. ''It still won't change a thing. We were meant for each other. When you stood in line at the Cinderella Ball and looked at me over Donato's head, you sensed the inevitable. And it terrified you. That's why you hid behind your mask.''

His perception devastated her. ''I've always known what I was doing and where I was going. I think it was mapped out by the time I was four. But with you...'' Her voice broke. ''I don't know anything.''

''And it frightens you.''

''Yes. I can't see the path, Marco. I don't know what to do next.''

''Close your eyes.'' He eased back, removing her arms from around his waist. ''Do it, Hanna. Close them.''

She trembled, confused by his request, more confused by the distance he'd put between them. ''They're closed.'' And she was alone in the darkness, more alone than she'd ever been in her entire life.

''Now reach out. I'm here.''

And he was. Her hands collided with his chest and she gathering his heat in her palms. Slowly she lifted her fingers to his face, following the strong, masculine lines, learning the taut planes and angles of her husband's features. She could picture them in her mind, with the analytical part of her nature. But touch gave them an added dimension, imprinting them on her soul.

Ever so gently she traced his mouth with her thumbs. And then she lifted on tiptoe and traced the sculpted lines with her lips. Her hands drifted down his neck and slipped beneath his collar, exploring the corded muscles beneath. Buttons fell unresisting beneath her fingers and his shirt parted. Still she didn't open her eyes, seeing more clearly with them closed than when they'd been open. To her utter amazement, her senses guided her, showing her the path she must take.

Following the narrow line of hair that plunged downward over his abdomen, her hands slipped to the clasp of his belt at the same instant as her tongue slipped between his lips. He opened to her, urging her inward. And yet he still didn't enclose her in his arms. He wanted to, she didn't doubt that for a moment. The desperate tension building across his shoulders and chest told her as much. But she knew he intended for her to take the lead, to set the pace of their lovemaking.

The rasp of his zipper vied with the harshness of his breathing. He tilted his head, his mouth plying hers with a fierce passion. He teased, he coaxed, he took, revealing his deepest desires with no more than that single kiss.

He wanted her, he merely waited for an invitation.

"Marco..." The air shuddered in her lungs as words deserted her. He'd always used the sweetest endearments when addressing her, why couldn't she say something equally as sweet and lyrical in return? "I swear I'm going to learn Italian after this."

His choked laugh was her only answer. But suddenly she needed his hands on her, needed to be in his arms. With slow deliberation, she trailed her fingertips from the powerful expanse of his shoulders downward along an impressive array of tautly bunched muscles, all the way to his wrists. Shackling him, she opened her eyes and wordlessly drew him into her embrace.

"Are you sure?" he asked.

"Positive."

"No regrets in the morning?"

"Why? Because I made love to my husband?"

His gaze turned molten. "I wondered when you'd get around to calling me that."

She started to answer, but found she couldn't. When she tried again, he stopped her words with his mouth. His hands landed on her shoulders and drifted relentlessly downward. Having received permission to touch her, he appeared intent on exploring every inch of her. No doubt she'd soon find herself thoroughly plucked—at least, she hoped so.

Her clothing proved a barrier swiftly removed. Next, he tackled his own clothes, sparing a precious few seconds to finish what she'd started. At long last, she stood before him without any of her protective guises, utterly vulnerable. He must have sensed her apprehension. No doubt it was painfully apparent. Any number of factors could have clued him in—from her gritted teeth, to her rigid stance and tightly balled fists, to the tremulous give and take of her breath. Nudity didn't lend itself well to artifice.

"I'm sorry, Marco," she said with a groan. "I don't know what's wrong. I want you, but—"

"Shh. It's all right. Close your eyes again," he instructed gently.

Her lashes fluttered downward, her trust absolute.

"Now just feel."

He touched her, sculpting her breasts before dipping his head to take the crests, one by one, into his mouth. An entirely different tension filled her, explosive and desperate. Her breath quickened and she balled her fists deep in his hair, returning his caresses with unabashed fervor. He cupped her bottom, lifting her closer. He was sheer male, and she'd never been so vitally aware of being a woman, of being intensely desired by a man.

"Please, Marco. Please don't let it end."

"End? Don't you know, *amor mio*? This is only the beginning."

He swept an arm beneath her knees and carried her to the bedroom. Moonlight filtered through the doorway leading onto the balcony, providing just enough light to see the bed— and to see the rose petals and downy feathers that covered the soft white sheet.

"Did you do this?" she asked, more deeply moved by such a romantic gesture than anything that had gone before.

His expression remained impassive, as though awaiting her reaction, bracing himself for the possibility that she might be upset. "I wanted tonight to be special for you."

She didn't doubt that for a minute. "It will."

He lowered her gently to the bed and followed her down. How could she have been apprehensive about making love to Marco? How could she have spent night after night hiding in her office instead of sharing moments like this? His weight pressed her into the sheets, the silken fluttering of feathers and flower petals stroking her back while her husband offered harder, hotter, more decisive caresses. The scent of roses mingled with a powerful, elemental odor, of man and woman and burning need.

"Don't be afraid," he whispered, stealing kiss after delirious kiss. "I won't hurt you."

Her head moved back and forth, feathers and petals twining in her hair. "I'm not sure I can promise the same."

"Let me worry about that." His hand stroked downward, cupping her breasts, kissing them, driving the tips into hard, painful peaks. But it wasn't enough, not nearly enough.

It took three tries to get the words out. "Please, Marco. Make love to me now. Don't wait any longer."

"I fully intend to, sweet. But slowly."

"No!" She squirmed beneath him, the brush of feather and petal and hard, firm hands almost too much to bear. "Fast. Go faster."

"Easy, love. We'll get there, I promise."

He palmed the back of her thighs, parting them. His fingers burned, eliciting a liquid warmth as he slipped inward. Touch built on determined touch, teasing her past mere arousal, driving her to a frenzy of need, a desperation for a completion only Marco could provide. She opened herself with utter abandon, lifting to welcome him in the most intimate of embraces. Gently he surged into her, filling her. And she knew that if she'd made love with any other man, it would have been wrong. There was a rightness to Marco's taking, to this ultimate completion of their wedding vows.

Then his lovemaking wasn't so gentle, but hard and driven. She gave everything within her. And he was there for her, too, making that night the most unforgettable of her life. With each delicious thrust the tension built, her muscles tensing in anticipation. A release swept down on her, storming every last defense, glorious in its beauty and explosive in its relentless power.

In that last instant, Marco covered her mouth with his in both benediction and promise. And in the calm that followed the storm, his words whispered between them, their conviction absolute.

"I love you, Hanna. I always have and I always will."

And in that moment, he became her husband in fact as well as name.

He loved her.

Hanna wasn't sure how many hours had passed since Marco had whispered that declaration. With all her heart, she wished she could offer a similar vow. But too much stood between them for her to make such an admission.

Rolling onto her side, she slipped her leg over his thigh, her toes tangling with his. "Marco, there's something I need to tell you."

He glanced at her, lifting an eyebrow. "Another secret, Hanna?"

"Yes. And this time you don't even have to use chocolate on me. I'll tell you of my own volition." Praying he wouldn't hate her, she lowered her head to his shoulder, knowing his reaction to her confession would be instantly communicated to her. "It's about the reason I attended the Cinderella Ball."

"Does it, by any chance, have something to do with the gentlemen sitting in your reception room when we first arrived in Hidden Harbor?"

"I'm afraid so."

"Did you marry me to stop your stepsons from matchmaking?"

She cleared her throat. "The thought did occur to me."

"And since your five-year deadline to find a husband was fast approaching...?"

"It seemed a logical move." She traced the triangle of hair matting his chest. "If it makes you feel any better, I didn't expect to find someone like you."

"That's all right, sweet. I didn't expect to find someone like you, either."

"Then, you're not mad?"

"No. As you said, you acted very... logically. Besides, I'd already figured out this particular secret."

"I thought you might have. But I also thought we should bring it out into the open, just in case." She moistened her lips. "I have one more confession."

"Heaven help us," he muttered. "What now?"

"I don't think logic has much to do with what's happened since," she admitted. In fact, it had absolutely nothing to do with her feelings for Marco. "I was going to pick someone like me. A charts-and-graphs type who wouldn't cause any problems."

Laughter rumbled against her cheek. "Sorry, *carissima*. Have I been troublesome?"

"I'll survive." She felt compelled to drop several totally illogical kisses across his chest. "But I thought I should be honest with you. Even though I was going to be very analytical about choosing a husband, I'm afraid I was seduced by a sweet-talking Italian Zorro. You might not fit into the lines of my various graphs. But I'm not sorry I married you."

"I appreciate that. I'm not sorry I married you, either." He tumbled her onto her back, kicking aside their covers, totally comfortable in his nudity—and hers, too, apparently. "Any other secrets you'd care to reveal?"

Not a chance! "Not right now, thanks."

"But soon?"

No! "Maybe," she replied cautiously. "We'll have to see how it goes."

"You're making this more difficult than it needs to be. You realize that, don't you?"

"I don't know what you're talking about," she lied.

He scooped up a handful of feathers and rose petals and scattered them across her body. "Have you heard the story of the swan princess?"

The abrupt change of subject caught her off guard, as did the whirlwind of silky caresses. "It's a children's tale, isn't it?"

"It's based on Tchaikovsky's ballet, *Swan Lake,* which in turn was based on an old German fairy tale." He chose the largest of the feathers that had landed on her and she shivered in anticipation. "Do you remember the story line?"

"Vaguely. Something about a prince having to rescue a princess who was disguised as a swan?"

''Not quite. In the ballet, an evil sorcerer turns the princess into a swan forced to live her life swimming in a lake of her mother's tears. Only in the depth of night can she reveal her true self and turn from swan to woman.'' He traced the outline of Hanna's mouth with the feather. ''One of those nights a prince comes upon her and they fall in love.''

''What about the spell?'' The feather drifted from her mouth across the tip of her chin and slowly, agonizingly downward. ''Or didn't it matter to him?''

''The prince vows to break the spell. But there's only one way to accomplish that.''

''Let me guess.'' Her voice sounded raw, strained with reawakened desire. ''It has something to do with true love.''

''You got it. He has to declare eternal devotion for her in front of witnesses. So the prince, who truly loves his swan princess, gives his solemn vow to break the spell by swearing his love at a ball.''

''A Cinderella ball?'' she managed to tease.

The feather paused in the hollow of her throat, threatening to drive her straight over the edge. "I have to admit, I hadn't thought of that."

"Well, maybe that was a different party," she allowed. "Go on with the story. Why do I get the impression it doesn't end at the ball?"

"Because it doesn't." He resumed his downward movement, stroking the feather across the tip of her breast. It peaked painfully beneath the soft caress and she needed every ounce of self-possession not to cry out. "You see, the evil sorcerer shows up at the ball with a woman he's disguised to look like the swan princess. When the prince declares his love for the wrong woman, the swan princess believes she's been abandoned for another, the prince's promise of eternal love an empty one. So she returns to the lake to die."

Hanna swallowed, desire ebbing. She didn't like this story. If she'd known it before the ball, she'd never have dressed the part. "Is that the end?"

"Not quite. The prince goes after the swan princess. In some versions, the story ends with the two dying together, throwing themselves in the lake so they'll be united forever through death. In others, the sorcerer creates a storm that drowns them. Still other versions have the prince finding the princess in time to break the spell.''

''How does he break it?'' She turned toward Marco, knocking the feather from his hand as she sought his warmth.

He pulled her close. ''By destroying the sorcerer.''

''I suppose that's easier than plucking the princess.''

Marco chuckled, the sound soft and intimate in the darkness. ''I can attest to that.''

''And killing off the bad guy satisfied her? She forgave him for getting his swans mixed up?''

''Oh, I suspect the prince had some apologizing to do.''

''Maybe even a bit of groveling?''

''No doubt. But she relents for a very good reason.''

''Which is?''

He kissed her, a slow, delicious joining of lips and tongue. ''Can't you guess?''

''They truly love each other?''

''Of course.''

"And their love was enough to overcome an evil sorcerer and the prince's small slip?"

"It was true love, Hanna."

He wasn't talking about *Swan Lake* anymore, and they both knew it. Tears burned, tears she refused to let fall. "Are you sure it's enough?"

"Very sure."

"There's a point to this, isn't there?" she asked tightly.

His sigh caressed her face. Gathering her in his arms, he carried her to the door of the balcony, a trail of rose petals and feathers scattered in their wake. He flung open the door and stepped outside, lowering her to the decking. The wooden planks were cold beneath her bare feet. The winds had changed direction, as Marco had forecast, sweeping in from the north and driving a wintery weather front before them. But she scarcely noticed. All she cared about was the man who held her, whose touch filled her with a desire so great, she shook with it.

"Dance with me, *carissima*. There's music here. Listen with your soul and you'll hear it."

And there, in the midst of a winter's night, she did hear. In Marco's arms, it became a symphony. A chilly breeze lifted her hair, coaxing stray feathers and rose petals into an airy ballet around them. As she drifted across the deck, secure in his arms, a solitary snow-flake swirled down to join the dance. Then another and another and another. It was the first snow of the season and Hanna knew in her heart that when Marco took her beneath the snow-flecked sky, it blessed their union.

Her husband's voice came to her as he filled her, the words soft, but driven by unassailable determination. "I don't know what sort of sorcerer enchanted you or what evil spell holds you, *amante mia,* but I will find a way to break it. Whatever it takes to end the secrets between us, I'll do. I swear it."

She closed her eyes, desperate to speak and unable to.

"I only ask one thing."

"What is it?" she managed to ask.

"Don't lose faith, Hanna. No matter what the future brings, promise to trust me."

Her response came without hesitation. "I promise, Marco. I'll always trust you."

But the wind howled as winter's first storm bore down on them, drowning out her voice.

The next several days were the most joyous Hanna had ever experienced. For the first time in her life, she became impatient with work, not to mention the narrow structure of her world. Making money had become boring. Fortunately, Marco knew precisely how to wreak havoc on structure, not to mention schedules and plans and lists and charts. He was particularly good at upsetting her carefully organized charts. But the one thing he excelled at was living life to the fullest. With him at her side, she found herself looking at the world from an entirely new perspective.

And what he showed her gave the breath of life to a heart and soul too long barren.

As the days passed, she vaguely heard Pru and her stepsons fussing in the background. At some point, she'd have to do something about them. But for now, her focus remained on Marco and the joy she felt whenever they were together. Even apart, she found work easier, less of a burden. But the moments she lived for were those first few seconds when the building emptied and grew quiet, as though holding its breath, waiting for the two lovers to bring it to life.

Then Marco would appear in the doorway. He'd look at her with those brilliant brown eyes, his gaze steadfast, the miracle of his love glittering with a passion she couldn't mistake. She'd fly across the room and into his arms and he'd strip away the outer artifice, revealing what she kept safely hidden from all others. Only then did she dare shed her feathers and become a real woman.

Was it love? She shied from the thought. It was too much, too soon. But one thing she did know. It was time to fling open the door and let Marco enter her inner sanctum. It was time to take him to the place it had all begun— where the evil sorcerer had first worked his spell.

CHAPTER NINE

THERE WAS SOMETHING ODD going on and
Marc couldn't quite put his finger on it. When
Hanna had suggested going for a drive before
dinner, he'd been willing enough. He was always delighted the times she suggested something contrary to her normal routine. But it
soon became apparent that she had a specific
destination in mind, along with a reason for
bringing him here.

"What is this place?" he asked as she
turned into an empty parking lot outside a tiny
steeple-topped building. "A church?"

"It used to be. It's deserted now."

"I can see that. So why are we here?"

He could see she struggled with her answer.
Was she getting ready to reveal another secret?
If so, this was a serious one. "It'll be easier
to show you," she finally said.

She climbed the sagging steps to the double
doors that fronted the small, vacant church.
Removing a large brass key from her pocket,

she inserted it in the lock. It took a bit of jiggling, but at last the bolt clanked home. Turning a knob stiff from disuse, she shoved the door open. Inside was a single huge room, simple and painfully empty. The pews and other religious accouterments had been removed long ago, leaving the chapel barren of life. As they walked inside their footsteps echoed into the rafters overhead, painfully harsh in the melancholy silence.

"There's a small meeting room with a kitchenette through here." She pointed to a door leading off the side of the chapel. "I stored everything there."

"Everything."

She nodded solemnly. "Yup. Everything."

The patient Salvatore, he reminded himself. "Lead the way."

The meeting room was spotless, a long table in the center of the room filled with tidy stacks of assorted canned goods, a dozen huge wicker baskets, checked napkins and various Thanksgiving decorations. "Want to help?" she asked casually.

"Help with what?"

"Preparing Thanksgiving baskets." A hint of uncertainty peeped out from behind her stoic expression. "It's a yearly tradition."

Tradition. Good. Traditions forged connections and united families. "Sure." He stripped off his jacket and tossed it aside. "Tell me what to do."

"Each basket gets one of everything. The turkeys are in the freezer. If you'll fill the baskets and arrange the contents so everything is attractive, I'll decorate each one."

"No problem." He grabbed the first basket and draped a large orange-and-yellow checked napkin in the bottom. Shooting her a curious glance, he tried to decide whether or not to probe. What the hell. It didn't look like she intended to volunteer the information. "Have you been doing this for long?"

"Ever since I was four. This is my second Thanksgiving on my own." She smiled, tying ears of Indian corn together with decorative feathers. "Except I'm not on my own anymore, am I?"

"Nope. Not even a little." He crossed to the freezer and removed a plastic-wrapped turkey, depositing it on top of the checked napkin. "So who was your previous helper?"

"Henry. Though to be honest, I was his helper. He'd been putting together baskets on the sly for years and years. He used this as his base of operations ever since they rebuilt the church in town...oh, twenty-five years ago, I guess."

Hanna hesitated, and Marc saw the secrets trembling on her lips, secrets desperate to be revealed. "And?" he prompted gently.

She shrugged. "And it's a good thing he did. Because otherwise I'd probably have died of exposure."

"Died...?" He forced himself to continue putting cans into the basket, struggling to regain his control, despite the fist-to-the-chest she'd just delivered. *Don't lose it now, Salvatore!* His wife was finally opening up to him and if he were very, very smart, he'd tread very, very lightly. "When was this?"

"Years ago. I was about three." Her composure was unassailable. So calm. So deliberate. So removed from what he instinctively sensed was a crucial moment in her life. "At least, they think I was three. Henry found me.

He'd come to put together the Thanksgiving baskets and... And there I was.''

''Just sitting on the church steps?''

Her smile held a painful incandescence. ''Right in the middle of the top one.''

''What happened to your parents?'' he probed.

She avoided his gaze, continuing to doggedly tie feathers to stalks of corn. ''I don't know.''

''You don't know? Or you don't want to know?'' He couldn't believe she could remain so remote when relaying one of the most horrendous stories he'd ever heard—a story in which she stood center stage. ''Hanna—''

The feathers seemed to burst from her hands, fluttering like wounded birds to the scarred wooden table. Her jaw set, perhaps to keep it from trembling. ''I was abandoned, okay?''

He fought to control his reaction, to dampen the words burning to be uttered. ''No, it's not okay,'' he said in impressively mild tones. ''Not for me and I suspect, not for you, either. Were your parents ever found?''

"No." With careful precision, she gathered up each feather and resumed her task. "No one knows who they were or why they…why they left me."

"Do you remember it?" he restrained himself to asking.

"Yes." The whisper-soft word was absolutely heartbreaking. "Though it's mostly sensations and shadowy images. Feelings."

"Bad feelings."

Silence.

"Feelings you've never gotten past."

He could hear the give and take of her breath—low and shallow, a desperately even filling of the lungs. But her hands betrayed her, trembling just enough so the feathers began to scatter across the table again. She tried to scoop them up, the helpless disarray unsettling to see in one so exacting.

Feathers, he thought, realizing it was the key. Hating himself for intentionally inflicting pain, he pushed one final time. "So the mother and father who were supposed to love you, abandoned you. They left the swan princess swimming in the middle of an empty lake. Alone and deserted."

The remoteness cracked, the expression in her hazel eyes so wounded, he thought the moment would forever scar his soul. It was a depth of agony beyond expression. Her face had turned pale against the blaze of curls, her silken skin stretched taut across fragile bones. Her mouth quivered ever so slightly and with an exclamation of fury, he shoved the basket aside and gathered his wife in his arms, holding her so tightly her helpless tremors knifed straight through him.

Babies take a lot of care, she'd said in the cottage before they'd made love. *They need time and attention. You can't just want them one minute and toss them aside the next when they become too much trouble.* She'd been the baby who'd been tossed aside. Had she spent the last twenty-some years trying not to be too much trouble for fear of being abandoned again? Is that why she held herself so remote and distant, terrified of love and all its inherent risks?

"Tell me," he ordered. "Tell me, *carissima,* so it's out in the open and not hidden away inside anymore."

"It was dark." The words tumbled free, fluttering as helplessly as the feathers had. "And cold. So cold."

He snatched up his coat and wrapped her inside, enclosing her in what little warmth he could provide. "They left you at night?"

Her hair caressed his chin as she shook her head, a gentle touch of vibrant life in the midst of deepest despair. "No. I think it was early in the morning, though it was still dark. They bundled me up and gave me a note. They said I shouldn't let go of the envelope, no matter what. And they told me to sit on the steps until the people came for church. It never occurred to them that the place had been deserted, that no one would be coming."

He swore, a vicious word that barely touched on his true emotions. "And then?"

"'Don't cry,' they said. 'Not one tear. Soon,' they kept repeating. 'Someone will show up soon.' But—"

Her voice broke and he prayed for strength, prayed he'd say the right thing. That somehow he could make it better. Deep down he knew nothing could do that. He was years too late for that. "You're not alone, anymore. I'm here, love."

Her hands slipped around his waist, clinging. "I remember the sun coming up across the fields. It looked huge and blood red. I thought the sky was on fire and I started trembling. It was probably from a combination of cold and fear. Still, it terrified me because I thought the shaking would make me drop the envelope." Her chin quivered and her voice dropped so low he had to strain to hear. "That's when I saw someone walking across the fields, filling the sky and putting out the fire."

"Henry?"

"Yes, Henry. He'd come to pick up the Thanksgiving baskets and deliver them. Instead, he found me. If he hadn't had such a generous heart... If he hadn't decided to use the old church as his base of operations..." Her humorless laugh held more than a hint of tears. "I never thought to ask if he delivered the baskets that year."

"*Dammit*, Hanna! To hell with the baskets. What happened after Henry found you?"

"He picked me up. Carefully. Like I might shatter if he were too rough. My hands were so cold, I couldn't even open them to give him that damned envelope. He finally pried it from my hand and read the note. And then—" Her breath shuddered in her lungs. "And then—"

"Finish it, sweetheart."

"He cried. I remember because I'd been told not to cry. And I hadn't. Yet, here was this great big man sitting on the steps with me on his lap and he was bawling like a baby. I felt so badly. Like I'd done something wrong. I kept patting his cheek and trying to tell him it was all right. Telling him what my parents had said, that people would come. But I was so cold, I doubt I made much sense. He just looked at me and shook his head, the tears dripping off his chin. I think that's the moment I knew my parents weren't coming back. I still didn't cry. Not that day and not since."

"You cried at the Cinderella Ball," he reminded gently. For some reason, it seemed a significant point.

"I *did* cry, didn't I?" Hanna remained silent for a long time. "I didn't think I could anymore,'' she murmured with something akin to wonder.

''What happened after Tyler found you? Foster care?''

''In a way. Henry kept me for awhile, but the authorities decided it wouldn't be proper for a widower with three strapping boys to raise me. Besides, he was a farmer whose crop had failed that year and he was struggling to make ends meet. It wasn't fair to burden him with another mouth to feed. Anyway, the town voted to keep me.''

''What do you mean they voted?''

''I mean everyone in Hidden Harbor got together to decide what to do about me. They voted to raise me.''

We found her. We're keeping her, Pru had said. Hanna had mentioned being raised by the town, or at least various ''suitable'' families in town. This explained it. ''That's what you started to tell me before, isn't it? On your birthday.''

''It's not really my birthday.'' She rested her cheek against his chest. ''The town fought over that, too. Some people wanted Thanksgiving to be my birthday. But my first parents said no, because it would hold too many sad memories. So they changed it to two weeks before.''

''No one knows the real date?''

''Someone knows,'' she whispered. ''Or they did once upon a time.''

Rage gripped him again, a rage as deep and overpowering as her pain. He fought to hide it from her. She sure as hell didn't need that on top of everything else. ''Your parents didn't even put that much information in the note they left?''

''Only my first name. They also said that they couldn't take care of me anymore and please find a willing couple to raise me.''

It took a moment before he had his temper under sufficient control to speak calmly. ''You know what I think?''

''What?''

He swept a tumble of curls from her cheek and cupped her chin, tilting her face up to his. Shadows darkened her eyes, shadows he'd give anything to erase. ''I don't think they could have been your real parents. I suspect you'd been left in their care. Perhaps your parents had died and they were appointed your guardians. They decided the responsibility was too much and—'' He waved a hand to indicate the town of Hidden Harbor. ''And here you are.''

Her mouth turned down in denial, but a wistful hope blossomed in her gaze. ''Do you think so?'' she asked skeptically.

''Yes, I do.'' His thumbs caressed her cheekbones and he spoke with unmistakable urgency. ''Listen to me, Hanna. We'll never know for sure, will we? So isn't it better to assume that strangers abandoned you, rather than your parents? If we can't be certain, why not assume the best, rather than the worst?''

Tears filled her eyes. Beautiful, emotional, heartrending tears. ''What if it's not true?''

''Do you have it within you to abandon a child you had borne?''

''*Never!*'' came her fierce response.

''Then neither could your mother and father. These were strangers, strangers without heart or soul who left you with a town who loved you and raised you to the best of their ability.'' He hesitated, something else occurring to him. ''Is that why you've never left Hidden Harbor? Because you owe them?''

"I owe the townspeople a debt I can never repay. But I haven't left because Hidden Harbor is my home. I don't want to live anywhere else."

He decided to leave it alone. "And Henry Tyler? Is that why you married him? Gratitude?"

"There were a lot of reasons."

"Such as his illness?"

"Yes."

"And helping to save his farm?"

"That, too."

"So now you're taking over Henry's Thanksgiving basket tradition, right?"

She shrugged. "It's a good cause."

"I know it is, sweetheart. I don't question that for a minute. But are you doing it out of a sense of obligation, because you're fulfilling a debt? Or are you doing it because it gives you pleasure to help others?"

She didn't understand. He could see it in the perplexed line that formed between her eyebrows. "Does it matter?"

"I'm beginning to think it does."

"I'm helping people who deserve help. What else is there?"

A lot more. And with luck, he'd show her. "What happens when you've finished preparing the baskets?"

"I call Pru and she arranges to have them picked up and delivered anonymously."

"You don't take care of it yourself?"

She looked at him as though he'd lost his mind. "That would sort of defeat the whole purpose of anonymous, don't you think?"

"Or perhaps you let Pru take care of it so you can hold people at a distance—the Dragonlady guarding the swan princess."

"Why would I want to do that?" He didn't answer, hoping she'd figure that out for herself. Sure enough, she released her breath in a sigh. "Okay, Marco. I get it. If I don't let people get too close, they can't hurt me. They can't abandon me emotionally."

He smiled tenderly. Score one for the good guys. "Makes it a bit tough to break the sorcerer's spell, don't you think?"

"Point taken," she conceded. "So what now?"

"Want to have some fun this year?"

His question intrigued her. "How?"

"I'll show you as soon as we're done with the baskets." Gently, he set her from him. "Get busy, wife. We have baskets to put together."

An hour later, a dozen baskets were filled to overflowing and they staggered to the car with them just as the sun sank into a stripped field of cotton.

"Where's the first stop?" he asked as they locked up the church and returned to the car.

"The Chase family over on Beech. Turn right at the first intersection. Their house is a ways down. I'll warn you when we get close."

Instead of driving directly up to the house, he parked the car around the corner where it wouldn't be seen. "I'll get the basket. You lead the way. Oh, and if you want this to stay anonymous, you'd better pull your hood up over that hair. It's a dead giveaway."

"It always has been," she grumbled, doing as he suggested.

The house Hanna indicated had definitely seen better days. The porch steps sagged and the peeling clapboard planks were in desperate need of a coat of paint. It looked like a house that could use a Thanksgiving treat. Signaling for his wife to follow, he crept up the steps and gently set the basket in front of the door.

"Ready?" he whispered. She watched him, wide-eyed and pink-cheeked, and he grinned at her excitement.

"What now?"

"Ring the doorbell."

"But they'll answer," she protested.

"Don't argue. Ring it."

Reaching past him, she stabbed the button. The instant she had, he grasped her hand and raced down the steps. Snatching her around the waist, he hauled her into a nearby clump of bushes. Crouching, he smothered her helpless laughter with his hand. A moment later, the front door opened and a scrawny boy of about ten appeared. Spying the basket, he crowed in excitement.

"Hey, Mom, come quick! Look what some-one left."

A heavily pregnant woman appeared, along with what seemed like an endless stream of children, every last one of them younger than the ten-year-old. They all gathered around the basket, oohing and ahhing over the contents. Hanna's laughter died and Marc removed his hand, glancing down at her. She watched the family, an odd expression on her face, almost as though she'd never realized how much her baskets meant to the families who received them.

Then it struck him. How could she? All the years she'd been doing this, she'd kept a safe distance, never touched by those she'd touched. But this time she witnessed the impact of her actions—saw and felt and understood the power of kindness extended and received. He remained quietly in the bushes until the Chase family had gathered up their gift and returned inside. And he continued to wait while his wife fully absorbed what had transpired.

Finally, she turned to him, her face glowing with a light that transcended explanation or expression—a light that eclipsed decades of pain. ''I never realized,'' she whispered. ''Thank you.''

''My pleasure, *cara,*'' he whispered back.

She tugged on his jacket. ''Come on. Let's go. I can't wait to deliver the next one.''

And so they went into the night, stopping at house after house, ringing the bell or pounding on the door, before scurrying into the bushes to watch as their gifts were welcomed with exclamations of joy and delight. At long last, they came to their final stop.

"This is Mother Jonathan's house. She was my first Mom," Hanna explained. "She couldn't have children, so she always called me her gift."

"It must have been hard giving you up."

"It was hard on both of us. But my second parents scheduled in regular visits, so I saw her every week." She brightened. "You'll get to meet her soon. I have Thanksgiving dinner with all my parents, which can get pretty filling. Fortunately Mother Jonathan cooks light. She always used to underestimate how much she should fix."

"You'd think she'd have figured it out after a while."

"You'd think, but she never did. Ever since Pop Jonathan died, Henry and I have delivered the baskets. I don't think Pops left her well off," Hanna confided. "Wait until you meet her. She's a real sweetie. Always happy and upbeat."

The Jonathan house was tiny and could also use a paint job. ''Perhaps we could hold a painting party,'' he suggested quietly as they approached the front door.

''I'll have Pru schedule it.''

''No need. I'll remember.'' He set down the basket and gestured toward the door. ''Do your stuff, princess.''

Grinning up at him, Hanna rapped sharply. Grabbing his hand, she raced down the steps with him and flew around an overgrown oleander. Peeking through the long green leaves, she slanted him a quick, eager glance. After a moment, the door opened, light streaming from the interior. A tiny figure shambled onto the porch.

''She looks old,'' Hanna murmured in concern. ''I never noticed before.''

Slowly, Mother Jonathan sank onto the top step of her porch beside the basket and gathered it in her arms.

Hanna stirred. ''What's she doing? Why isn't she taking it inside? Is something wrong?''

''No, sweet. Something's very right.''

Clutching the basket, Mother Jonathan rocked slowly back and forth, cradling the contents to her chest. Words whispered through the crisp night, but they were too far away to hear them clearly. But the broken tone suggested they were words of desperate thanks. At long last, she climbed to her feet and turned toward the door. Beside him, Hanna froze and he knew she'd seen what the light reflected, just as he had.

Tears.

"She's crying." She started around the bush, fighting him when he stopped her. "Marco, we have to do something."

"We did do something, Hanna," he explained gently. "We provided her with a Thanksgiving dinner she couldn't have otherwise afforded. And we allowed her to keep her dignity intact."

She rounded on him, helplessness vying with a fury directed squarely at herself. "She didn't have enough food. I didn't realize. I swear, I didn't. I'd have done something. I'd have helped her."

"She has enough now. You gave that to her."

"But I didn't do enough!" she practically shouted. "I'd have known if I hadn't been so preoccupied with that damned business. If I hadn't been so determined to—"

She broke off, but the unspoken words scorched the air between them. *Determined to hold myself at a safe distance, to hold people at a safe distance.*

The tears came at last, harsh, painful tears. Tears she'd kept locked inside for twenty-four long years. He caught her close, holding her with silent promise. "You did good, love," he soothed. "You did fine."

"No! No, I'm supposed to—" Her breath hiccuped in her throat. "To take care of her like she took care of me." She stared up at Marc, begging for an answer. "Why didn't I? Why?"

Sorrow etched deep lines in his face. "It's your life, Hanna. It's your choice. Lists. Schedules. Charts. All the things that help keep you safe and distant from others. Or people. Nosy, messy, inconvenient, occasionally heartbreaking, but filled with love. It's your decision."

She shook her head, panic dimming the color of her eyes. "Marco—"

"I understand this is difficult for you. I understand why you're afraid to allow love to touch you." Hanna turned from him, but he could see the flicker of her lashes that revealed she was still listening. "But if you close the door on people, you truly will be alone and deserted, destined to swim in that lake of tears by yourself for the rest of your life. You'll condemn yourself to forever being the swan, instead of transformed into the woman you were meant to become."

He didn't dare say more. Either she would take his words to heart and open herself to others. Or he'd lose her. Permanently.

And there wasn't a damned thing he could do about it.

Hanna spent the next two days giving serious consideration to Marco's comments. He was right and she knew it. She grimaced. Of course, that didn't make it any easier to do as he'd suggested. She'd spent her entire life protecting herself from hurt, her fear of abandonment governing her every decision. But with Marco...

She closed her eyes and faced the undeniable truth. From the moment she'd seen him, she'd been unable to hold herself at a distance. He'd dropped into her life with all the flair and grace and passion of the character he'd imitated at the Cinderella Ball, breaching her defenses with a simple look

But clearly, his patience would soon run out. Either she trusted him or she didn't. Either she lo—

A tapping at the office door interrupted her thoughts. "Hanna, girl? We need to talk," Pru announced.

Hanna released a silent sigh and continued to stare broodingly from one of the windows fronting her office building. "Not now."

"Yes, right now. The boys and I have something to tell you."

"The boys?" Hanna turned, surprised to find herself hemmed in by her secretary and three overgrown sons. "What's this about?" she asked suspiciously.

Jeb took the lead. "It's about Salvatore. And Hanna..." He hesitated, his expression unusually solemn. "It's not good."

CHAPTER TEN

HANNA CLOSED HER EYES. *Not now. Oh, please, not now!* "Look, boys, you're going to have to learn to get along with him. He's my husband and I—" She stilled. "And I—"

It hit then. Hit with a force that provoked tears of shocked wonder. *And I love him!* Why hadn't she realized before? All the signs were there. Her reaction whenever he came near. Her ability to reveal her deepest secrets, secrets she'd kept hidden from every other person. It also explained her desperation to change a lifetime of habits. More than anything, she wanted to open herself to Marco, to share the future he offered.

"Mother T?" Janus asked.

She stared at them in wonder. "It's Mother S now."

Josie exchanged worried looks with his brothers. "Are you all right?"

"Oh, dear heaven," she whispered. "I love him. I *do* love him."

When had that happened? When they'd delivered Thanksgiving baskets? No, before then. When he'd danced with her, making love beneath a snow-filled sky? No. Not then, either. She hadn't been ready to admit to the feelings, though they'd been there nonetheless. Perhaps when she'd gotten drunk on chocolate and he'd so tenderly put her to bed? She closed her eyes, facing the truth.

She'd fallen in love with her husband when she'd met his gaze over the head of a personable three-year old. Her future had been decided when he'd lowered a scrap of silk on the end of a sword and vaulted onto the bench beside her. And it had been sealed when he'd kissed her, finding a heart she'd thought too cold to respond to the warmth of love and releasing a soul trapped in sorrows of the past.

"This is *not* good," Josie informed his brothers. "We're too late."

"Damned gigolo."

"A lying thief, that's what he is," Pru pronounced, folding her arms across her chest. "First he tricks Hanna into marriage and now he's going to ruin her business."

Hanna held up her hands to still the rapid-fire discussion. "You're giving me a headache. Could you please slow down and tell me—in an orderly fashion—what the *hell* you're talking about?"

"For starters, we're talking about this." Pru tossed a well-known financial magazine onto the desk beside Hanna. "Remember it?"

"Sure. It's the issue containing the article they did about me."

"Right. The one that describes you as the 'financial genius of Hidden Harbor.' The silly columnist blabbed about how there's not a resident in the county who hasn't benefitted in some way from your money know-how. That article made you so popular, we had to beat the suitors off with a stick."

"Not that she wanted them beat off," Josie allowed. "What with her five-year goal, and everything."

Hanna gaped at him. "You...you *knew* about my goal?"

"Hell, Mother T." He gestured toward where her chart had once hung. "We can read. We even know how to turn pages and read stuff we weren't supposed to. Why did you think we kept dragging by all those men? It wasn't for our benefit, that's for damn sure. We thought it was what you wanted.''

So much for her stupid charts. ''Is there a point to this?'' she asked through gritted teeth.

''The magazine was in Zorro's briefcase,'' Pru hastened to explain. Her mouth thinned. ''Bet you didn't even realize he had a brief-case, did you? He hid that well—in the down-stairs closet, to be exact. What sort of salesman carries around a briefcase, I ask you?''

''Lots of salesmen carry around brief-cases!'' Hanna snapped.

''With an article about you hidden inside?''

''Do you get it?'' Jeb asked, as though to someone without the mental faculties to add two and two. ''He knew who you were.''

Janus nodded. ''*Before* you married.''

''That's ridiculous. It was a masked ball. He didn't see me until after we'd—'' No, that was wrong. She'd just been thinking about their original meeting. He'd seen her face when she'd first arrived. In fact, he'd scrutinized her quite closely, making her so uncomfortable she'd hidden behind her mask again. She shook her head. ''No. You're mistaken.''

"Did he see you unmasked before coming on to you?" Josie asked.

"Yes, but—" She glared at the four. "He is *not* a gigolo."

"Really? Well, he's not a salesman either," Pru retorted.

"How do you know?"

"He's an investor. Or perhaps I should say, he invests *other* people's money. I doubt he risks any of his own." Pru held up her hand. "And before you ask, I know because I did a little digging."

Her words had a familiar ring. What had Marco told her at the Cinderella Ball about his job? *What I seduce from them is money. As much as they'll give me.* A sick feeling crept into the pit of her stomach. "Oh, no."

"It gets worse," Jeb pronounced. "He wasn't even a guest at this Cinderella Ball Pru told us about. He just happened to be visiting the Beaumonts that particular weekend."

"Which means he wasn't investigated like the other guests," Pru added.

Hanna rallied. "So? He mentioned that to me. At least, he mentioned that he was a friend of the Beaumonts. As far as I'm concerned, that's a recommendation, not a condemnation.''

''He was there on a sales call, not as a friend,'' Pru hammered home. ''And seeing you, he took advantage of the perfect opportunity.''

''I thought you said he wasn't a salesman!''

''Okay, fine. He was there on an *investment* call, trying to wheedle money out of rich folk. The point is… He didn't plan to marry until he saw you. He knew who you were and took a chance. And may I add, it was a chance that's reaped a bountiful harvest.''

''Oh, for—'' Hanna planted her hands on her hips. ''If he's all you say, why hasn't he approached me about making an investment in his company?''

Pru snorted. ''Canny devil. He's trying to get you to fall in love with him first. Feeding you chocolates.''

Janus nodded in agreement. ''Bringing you flowers.''

''Kidnapping you so he can have his wicked way with you,'' added Josie.

''He's my husband,'' Hanna pointed out gently. ''He's allowed to have his wicked way with me.''

"Oh, yeah?" Jeb exchanged significant glances with his brothers. "If he's the perfect husband for you, why was he kissing another woman? Explain *that* if you can."

Hanna fought for air. "What did you say?"

Pru shot Jeb a quelling glance. "I'm sorry, Hanna girl. I meant to break it to you gently. The boys saw Salvatore."

"Kissing a woman," Janus interrupted. "And by the look of things, she wasn't his sister."

"Marco doesn't have a sister," Hanna retorted automatically. The sick feeling in her stomach expanded, creeping relentlessly toward her heart. "But it couldn't have been him. You must have been mistaken."

Pru nodded. "That's what I thought. So I went to check for myself. Figured these three knuckleheads couldn't get it straight if a line were painted for them to follow."

"Hey!"

"But sure enough. I saw them with my own two eyes. Your husband, one well-built blonde and a whole lot of lip action." Pru sighed. "There wasn't any mistake, Hanna. I'm sorry."

The door opened behind them and Marco stepped into the room. His comprehension was instantaneous. ''Am I interrupting some-thing?'' he asked with a mildness belied by the deadly glitter in his eyes. Their gazes locked, clashing without words.

''Want us to take him out?'' Jeb offered. ''He might have thrown me once, but I'll bet if the three of us jump him all together, we can do some serious damage.''

''No, thank you.'' What had happened to her voice? Why did it sound so wounded, so grating? After all, she hadn't really expected her marriage to work, had she? ''If you'll ex-cuse me, I have to talk to my hus— To Marc.''

Marco folded his arms across his chest, waiting with a watchful expression as the four filed past him, no doubt giving him the benefit of more than one acidic look on their way out. ''What's this about, Hanna?''

Not *amor mio* or *carissima* or *moglie mia*. Not even a tenderly said ''sweet.'' Just plain old Hanna. ''I need to ask a few questions.''

''I see. You need to…or is it the boys who need to?''

She lifted her chin and fixed him with a cool gaze. "They brought some information to my attention."

"And you believe whatever it is they said." It wasn't a question.

"They weren't lying, if that's what you're asking."

"Right." For the first time in the weeks she'd known him, a cynical light chilled the warmth in his brown eyes. "Let's get this over with, shall we?"

She steeled herself to deal with whatever the next few minutes revealed. "Did you know who I was before we married?"

"How would I know that?"

She indicated the damning evidence sitting so innocently on her desk. "There's a story on me in there."

"Interesting," he said softly. "I thought I left that particular issue in my briefcase."

"You did."

Winter descended, turning his features to ice, as hard and barren and unassailable as a glacier-stripped mountaintop. "Not nice, Hanna. I'd have thought better of you."

She didn't bother to correct his assumption. After all, Pru was her secretary, and therefore her actions were Hanna's responsibility. "Is it true? Did you know who I was?"

"And if I did?"

"Did you marry me so I'd invest in your business? Are you in financial trouble?"

His features went absolutely impassive, every thought and emotion eclipsed by darkness. "You have all the answers. You tell me. Have I been faking my feelings for you these past several weeks?"

No! a faint, desperate voice shrieked. But it was overridden by a louder voice, one filled with so much pain, she couldn't ignore it. "You were seen kissing another woman. Who is she, Marc? Or does it matter?"

He didn't move, his stillness absolute. But his rage was so great, it impacted on every sense. She could even smell it, the odor burning like sulphur. "I warned you this day would come."

"If you'd just explain—"

"Explain!" He took a step toward her, one that had her falling back in dismay. "You had a choice, wife," he whispered. *"You had a choice!"*

"You don't understand. They saw you with her! And they found the magazine in your—"

He sent the glossy journal skittering off the table with a powerful sweep of his hand. "And you believed them."

Instead of me. The words went unsaid, but echoed so loudly, she flinched. "I want to believe you. Just tell me—"

"No. Either you trust me or you don't."

The silence blanketing the office was so absolute it seemed to suck the very air from the room.

He retreated, withdrew physically and emotionally, leaving her totally alone. "Swim, little princess," he advised, his lyrical accent building with each word. "Hug your feathers close and swim for all you're worth. Because even with wings, you're not going to fly. Not when fear keeps you earthbound."

With that, he turned and walked to the door. "Marco, wait!" Cold was seeping into her veins, stealing the warmth she'd known for too brief a time. "Where are you going? What are you doing?"

He didn't turn around. "I'm going to make sure your worst fear comes true," he explained very, very gently. "I'm going to leave you."

He walked out of her office without another word and Hanna realized that what she'd experienced at the tender age of three was nothing compared to this. All those years ago she'd been left to find love. But this time the love she'd found had left her.

Her knees failed and the tidy, colorless rug she'd chosen with such care rose up to catch her.

"It didn't work," Marc retorted in a rare burst of fury. "Can we leave it at that?"

Luc shook his head. "I'm not sure we can. At least, not until you explain what happened."

"You sent Stefano after me because of this damned board meeting. That's what happened. I came. End of story."

"Without your wife and snapping like a rabid dog at everyone who comes within ten feet of you and basically acting like a total *cafone*."

Marc's jaw jutted out. "Yes."

"Uh-huh." Luc stared at his brother, perplexed. "Stef said some overgrown giant tried to take his head off while he was in Hidden Harbor. What was that about?"

"Next time tell him to keep his hands off the local women."

Luc started to say something, then stopped, his eyes narrowing. Comprehension swiftly followed. "Aw, hell. They thought he was you. *Cretino!* Didn't you explain? Didn't you introduce Stefano to them?"

Marc glared, refusing to answer.

"Never mind," Luc said with a sigh. "I can see you didn't. I assume there was a case of mistaken identity?"

"You might say that."

"And your sweet wife, in true wifely fashion, stripped a layer or two off your hide."

"She's a redhead," Marc acknowledged with a shrug, as though that explained everything. "And it wasn't just the other woman. She thought I married her for financial gain, as well."

"She thought *you* needed her money?" Luc held up a hand, fighting to stifle his laughter. "No, let me guess. You didn't tell her who you were any more than you explained about Stef. Why didn't you show her that article on the Salvatores? The one in last month's business journal?''

''She has the magazine! If she'd bothered to read further than the spread they did on her little town, she'd have seen the article for herself.'' Marc paced the room, his restless movements too much even for the generous proportions of Luc's office. ''Did she think so little of our marriage? Of the vows we made to each other? Salvatores only marry for love. What further proof does she need than that?''

''I don't suppose you bothered to mention that part of our family tradition?'' Luc grimaced. ''No, never mind. She wouldn't have believed you any more than Grace believed me.''

''I shouldn't have to tell her! How could she think I'd touch another woman after being with her?''

''I don't know...'' Luc said with more than a touch of irony. ''Maybe because you have a twin brother intent on seducing anything remotely resembling the opposite sex, a brother who happens to be a dead ringer for you. A brother you, no doubt, conveniently failed to mention.''

Marc folded his arms across his chest, refusing to consider he was being the least mule-headed. ''What's your point?''

The furious stream of Italian that followed was offered in a scathing tone of voice and punctuated with more than a few curses. Marc sighed, ignoring his brother's outburst.

Ah, little swan princess. We came so close to breaking the spell. If only you could have trusted me. If only you could have allowed love into your life.

''Marco? Are you even listening to me?''

''Let it alone, Luc,'' he said wearily. ''Sometimes love isn't enough.''

''You're giving up? Just like that? You questioned Hanna's attitude toward her wedding vows... Do they mean so little to *you* that you won't fight to make your marriage work?''

How odd that pain could be so unbelievably intense, and yet he could still speak. ''You don't understand. If I force her, she'll never learn to fly on her own. And unless she's brave enough to escape the lake, she can't break the spell.''

Luc thrust his hands through his hair. "I get it now. I don't know why it didn't occur to me before. She's not the one who's crazy. *You* are."

Marc nodded morosely. "Yes, I'm afraid you're right. My wife isn't crazy, she just can't shed her feathers, poor little swan. I'm the insane one." *Insanely, helplessly, passionately in love with the sweetest swan princess ever to be enchanted.*

"What are you doing?" Pru demanded. "Where are you going?"

Hanna confronted her secretary, the light of battle glittering in her eyes. "I'm going to find my husband."

"For that you need three suitcases?"

"I needed three for all my stuff. At least, all the stuff I'll need."

Pru stared in dismay. "You're not coming back, are you?"

"Not without Marco. And not unless it's what he wants, too. After his welcome here, I suspect that's highly doubtful."

"But, the money. The other woman—"

"I didn't give a damn about the money. As for the other woman..." Memories swirled like feathers on a breeze. Beautiful, soul-stirring memories. Her jaw set. "There's got to be an explanation. He loves me. He'd never betray that love. Not Marco."

"But you're going to get that explanation, right? Before you go back to him?"

"No."

Pru's mouth dropped open. "No? What do you mean no? Have you lost your mind?"

There will come a day when you'll be forced to make a choice between your head and your heart, Marco had warned, once upon a time. *Your head will tell you to doubt. To run. And that's when you'll face an irrevocable decision. You'll have to trust. When everyone and everything around you is screaming for you to doubt, you'll have to take that leap of faith. Make the wrong choice and you'll regret it for the rest of your life.*

Well she'd faced that choice and failed miserably. She wouldn't fail again. "I have no idea who you saw, but it wasn't Marco." Not after what they'd shared. It couldn't have been. Her lips trembled. Why hadn't she realized that from the start?

"I'm telling you, it was," Pru protested. "I saw him with my own two eyes."

"No." And that said everything. Hanna scrutinized her suitcases. "You know what? I don't need any of this stuff."

"But—"

"Have a good Thanksgiving, Pru. Thanks for what you've done." Picking up her purse, she looked around for a final time. "Give everyone my love, will you?"

Her secretary hesitated for a minute before surrendering to the inevitable. "Okay, Hanna girl. If that's how you feel, you have my support. But I suspect the boys aren't going to be happy about this."

"Actually, we will," Josie interrupted. "If this is what Hanna really wants."

She spun around. Her three "boys" were lined up by the stairwell. She gave them a misty smile. "It's what I want. *He's* what I want."

Jeb opened his arms. "Then give us a hug goodbye."

She flew into his embrace. "Thank you for everything you've done."

"No. We thank you. We know if it weren't for you—" He swallowed. "We can never repay all you've done for our family. Thank you, Mother—Signora Salvatore. Have a good life."

"I—"

Jeb shook his head, stopping the emotional words before they could be uttered. "There's nothing more to say, Hanna. We have a car waiting downstairs to take you to the airport."

"If you hadn't decided to go, we were going to make you," Janus added.

Josie grinned. "There's even an escort. I think half the town turned out to see you off."

"They...they knew I'd leave?"

"They knew. And every last one is cheering you on."

It was all she needed to hear. She left the reception area without a backward glance. *Marco!* she thought, breaking into a trot. Fear blossomed, but a far different kind than the one she'd lived with for so many years. It was a desperate fear that she'd waited too long, left her decision until too late. The trot became a dash, the dash a sprint, the sprint a flat-out run. Her hair tumbled down her back, the color a flag of burning determination. She ran, ran as swiftly as she could. Racing faster and faster and faster....

And then she flew, unstoppable, soaring high and free, winging steadfastly toward her heart's desire.

"Excuse me, Madam. But you can't go in there! Mr. Salvatore is in a meeting and can't be interrupted."

"Watch me!" came a determined voice. It was a sweet, warm, familiar voice, one that had haunted Marc's dreams from the moment he'd first heard it. A voice that gave him such joy, it threatened to totally unman him, despite his family's presence.

An instant later, the door slammed open and the woman who held his heart in her tender care stepped across the threshold. He wasn't in her line of sight, since he'd abandoned the conference table to pour himself a drink. But he could see her and what he saw brought a broad smile to his mouth.

She halted inside the doorway, straight and determined, her stance daring anyone to interfere with her goal. Her hair poured down her back in loose, fiery curls that quivered with vitality. Gone were the dark, protective dresses that she'd used to conceal the inner woman. Instead, she stood before the Salvatores in shimmering gold, a color he didn't doubt echoed the distinctive blaze in her hazel eyes.

He knew then that his swan princess had been transformed.

Her glance swept those seated at the conference table, keying in on Stefano. ''Dammit, Marco, we have to talk,'' she announced, stalking toward him.

She'd only taken three steps before flinching back. If she'd been a creature of the wild, he'd have seen the hackles rise at the nape of her neck. As it was, she froze, every muscle tensed in an instinctive fight-or-flight reflex.

''You're not Marco,'' she stated with absolute certainty.

Luc inclined his head, clearly impressed. ''No, he's not, Miss—'' He regarded her questioningly.

''Salvatore. *Mrs.* Salvatore. Now where's my husband?''

''Right here.''

Hanna spun around, her breath hitching. She took a quick step in his direction before hesitating, no doubt uncertain about her reception. "Let me warn you. I've been taking a crash course in Italian."

A laugh broke from him. No wonder he loved her. "Anticipating a fight?"

She folded her arms across her chest. "Is there any doubt?"

"None." He regarded her with mock innocence. "Here for a visit?"

"No. I'm here to stay." Her chin inched upward. "And to prove it, I brought you something."

"And what would that be?"

She opened her purse and removed the mask she'd worn to the Cinderella Ball. It was rather the worse for wear. The feathers were crushed, the stems snapped so they drooped pathetically. "No more hiding." She ripped the mask in half, feathers erupting into the air. She flung the tattered ruins at his feet. "I trust you, Marco. I should have stood up for you when Pru and the boys made their accusations."

"Yes, you should have. Why didn't you?"

"Because I was afraid." Her chin quivered ever so slightly. "So I tried to use logic to cover up my fear instead of listening with my heart."

"Are you telling me you're not afraid anymore?"

"No." Defiant. Absolute. Conviction blazed in every line of her face.

Now for the important question. He eyed her gravely. "How do I know that you won't be afraid next time something similar happens?"

"Because I'm going to tell you my last secret." She gestured toward his family. "Right here, in front of everyone. That way all the fears will be out in the open."

And thereby shedding the last of her feathers. A small smile played at the corners of his mouth. "You think that's enough?"

"I hope it will be."

"Then tell me, *carissima*."

She took a deep breath. "I love you."

"That's it?" He lifted an eyebrow, pretending to be less-than-impressed. "That's your secret?"

She clenched her hands together. "No. I'm hoping you might have already figured that out for yourself. My secret is..." She swallowed convulsively. "My secret is that I've never said those words to anyone before in my entire life."

It took a minute for the impact of her words to sink in. When they had, he glanced over her shoulder to his brothers and jerked his head toward the door. They took the hint. For the first time in their collective lives, they didn't say a single word, but simply filed from the room.

"You've never told anyone you love them before?" he rapped out.

"Never. Not Henry. Not the boys. Not...not any of my parents." Tears glistened in her eyes, turning the greens and golds to the color of newborn leaves unfurling beneath a spring-bright sun. "But I better warn you that that's going to change. I can't just love you, Marco, although I'll love you more than anyone else. I need to love others, too. Jeb and Janus and Josie. And Pru."

He sighed. "Pru?"

"Yes, Pru. And...and Mother Jonathan." A tear spilled onto her cheek, unchecked and unashamed. "Especially Mother Jonathan.

Please, Marco. I don't want a trial marriage anymore. I want it to be real.''

He didn't need to hear any more. He opened his arms to her, gathering her close. ''I love you, Hanna.''

''And I... *Ti amo, Marco.*'' She gazed up at him with an expression so open and clear, he couldn't doubt her final fears had been banished. ''Am I forgiven?''

''You were forgiven even when you doubted,'' he assured gently.

It took her a moment to recover enough to respond. ''I love you so much. I didn't think it was possible.'' The tears overflowed. ''Not for me.''

''It is possible. Not for you, but for us.'' He dipped his head, whispered against her lips, ''Welcome home, wife. Welcome home.''

And then Marc took her mouth in both benediction and promise, holding her as though he'd never let go. The future spread before them shining with joyous promise. From deep in Hanna's hair, a feather drifted free, spinning to the floor in silent acknowledgment.

At long last, the spell had been broken.